PENGUIN BOOKS

The Mummy Diaries

Rachel Johnson writes for (among others) the *Daily Telegraph*, the *Spectator* and the *Evening Standard*. She is married with three children and lives in Notting Hill Gate.

The Mummy Diaries

Or How to Lose Your Husband, Children

and Dog in Twelve Months

RACHEL JOHNSON

PENGUIN BOOKS

PENGUIN BOOKS
Published by the Penguin Group
Penguin Books Ltd, 80 Strand, London WC2R 0RL, England
Penguin Group (USA) Inc., 375 Hudson Street, New York, New York 10014, USA
Penguin Group (Canada), 10 Alcorn Avenue, Toronto, Ontario, Canada M4V 3B2
(a division of Pearson Penguin Canada Inc.)
Penguin Ireland, 25 St Stephen's Green, Dublin 2, Ireland
(a division of Penguin Books Ltd)
Penguin Group (Australia), 250 Camberwell Road, Camberwell, Victoria 3124,
Australia (a division of Pearson Australia Group Pty Ltd)
Penguin Books India Pvt Ltd, 11 Community Centre,
Panchsheel Park, New Delhi – 110 017, India
Penguin Group (NZ), cnr Airborne and Rosedale Roads, Albany,
Auckland 1310, New Zealand (a division of Pearson New Zealand Ltd)
Penguin Books (South Africa) (Pty) Ltd, 24 Sturdee Avenue,
Rosebank 2196, South Africa

Penguin Books Ltd, Registered Offices: 80 Strand, London WC2R 0RL, England

www.penguin.com

First published by Viking 2004
Published in Penguin Books 2005

2

Printed in England by Clays Ltd, St Ives plc

To my mother, the painter Charlotte Fawcett Johnson Wahl

I would like to thank the two First Ladies of newspapers, Sarah Sands and Veronica Wadley, Juliet Annan – 'MeJulie' – of Viking Penguin, my very patient agent Peter Strauss, Rachel Simhon of the *Daily Telegraph*, Julia Johnson, and, of course, Ivo, Ludo, Milly, Oliver and Coco (but not necessarily in that order).

January

January

We were all in the kitchen; I was clearing up after the children's supper, and my husband came home early. He hugged all the children in turn, reserving his most lingering embrace for the puppy, then turned to me with a strange light in his eyes – as if scanning a distant savannah for migrating wildebeest.

'I'm going to Africa,' he said. 'For work,' he added rapidly, as if I would otherwise assume that he and Iman were off on an undercover expedition to find the source of the Blue Nile or the fleshpots of Zanzibar.

'Are you?' I said, because I had by this stage cleared up supper, and was supervising the children's homework while threading a new pair of Persil-white shoelaces into my daughter's grubby trainers. 'Great! When?' I continued, after a prolonged pause during which I kept trying and failing to push the lace through the mud-caked slit in the nylon.

'Tomorrow,' he said. 'I'm afraid I'm going to miss half-term.'

The children's faces fell, and I tried to summon the spirit of the Blitz for their sakes. 'It's all right, children, we'll have a lovely time on Exmoor – Granddaddy and Jenny will be there and all the Johnson cousins are coming,' I rallied them. 'When will you be back?' I aimed, in more direct tones, at my husband.

'Not for a couple of months, I'm afraid,' he said.

That news, I have to confess, did absorb my attention for a second or two (like many husbands, mine claims I never listen to him nor answer his questions. This is not strictly accurate. I do hear him, but I tend to answer him in my head).

After the wails from the children had subsided, he said that not only would he be away for the next two-and-a-half months, but he would also not be returning to Blighty at all during his African tour, which has led me to embark, this week, on a long-overdue, royal-commission-style review of my domestic arrangements.

Which are as follows. Since around the start of the school year I have acquired a pet (a glossy black Labrador-collie puppy, Coco, of which an awful lot more later, I'm afraid – we're smitten), waved my nanny goodbye and lost my husband to the Kenyan general election. So I am 'flying solo' until the end of term.

(Oh yes, which reminds me of the last time I was flying solo, in Brussels. I once let slip to my landlord, a courtly Belgian baron, that my husband was working three days a week in London and Eurostarring between the two capitals. He looked at me and his face broke into an appreciative smile for the first time – we had so far shared only sticky discussions about the villa's volcanic drainage problems, referred to as '*la vidange*', up until my happy revelation.

'*Mais félicitations, madame*,' he purred, gallantly

air-kissing my wrist. Then, he was so moved by my words that he broke into English – another first for us. 'Many, many Belgian women, *madame*, I assure you, would envy you such a *tellement parfait* arrangement.')

Well, I can't pretend I am as *enchanté* as a proper Frenchwoman would be by such a prolonged stint of grass widowhood, but I am taking steps to make it tolerable.

My cleaner now comes, if not daily, a spoiling three times a week, and I write out her large cheque on Friday with deep gratitude. I have an adorable team of midriff-revealing teenage babysitters who allow me to leave the confines of my house every so often. My beloved mother comes to stay for one night a week, and has taken my daughter's hamster, Honey, off my hands, having rechristened it Honeyballs, after unilaterally resolving certain gender issues.

Soon, I hope to be in a position to tell you all about my trip to Wimbledon to pick up a new au pair from a Latin-American convent.

But, meanwhile, I have a serious crisis on my hands. It concerns Coco, the puppy.

It has proved not enough for my daughter that I have bowed to her dearest wish and agreed to have a puppy. Now, of course, my daughter's newest dearest wish is for the puppy to have puppies. (In this, she is displaying perfect consistency. After watching *Parent Trap* for the third time, I found her in tears. 'What is it, darling?' I asked. 'I don't just want a baby sister any more, Mummy,' she sobbed. 'I want an *identical twin* baby sister. Please!') As she – Coco the puppy, not the imaginary, longed-for identical twin for Milly – is already nine months old, the moment when all the dogs in the communal garden will be tunnelling into our house to 'marry' Coco will soon be upon us.

There are, at the last count, four 'intact' male dogs on the shared garden and all of them have shown lively interest in Coco, who is – though I say so myself – the Naomi Campbell of mongrels, with long black legs and eyes like molten caramel. And all the dogs' owners – my Notting Hill neighbours and friends – have made it crystal clear that any issue from any union will be my responsibility, and mine alone.

PS This really is the last straw. My husband has telephoned from Kenya – for the first time since he left – with the sole purpose of instructing me not to spay Coco under any circumstances. Having issued that command, he said the call was very expensive and rang off. Did I really sign up for this? And how on earth will my new au pair – *Dios mío!* – cope with Coco's litter as well as mine?

According to my American corporate-wife friend Helen, who helps keep me abreast of key developments in the parenting and personal-growth industries, I am 'nanny-phobic'. She made this intergalactic pronouncement after I had a long whinge about how tough it was being in so many places at the same time (last week there were two parents' evenings on consecutive days, scheduled in the 5–7 p.m. meltdown slot, coinciding with my daughter's art lesson and my turn to do the school run back from Hampstead). And I still haven't been to the Latin-American convent in Wimbledon yet to choose an au pair.

'I don't get it,' she interrupted after I had been rabbiting in this vein for some time. 'Get the nanny to give the kids tea, while you meet with the teachers. And trade days with another mom on the run.'

Now, I cannot pretend that I dislike the next line in my chosen script.

Delivering it, for some reason, makes me feel like a superior, almost saintly, being.

'But, Helen, I don't have a nanny,' I say, my brave sigh just hinting at the sacrifices I am making in my noble aspiration to be a more hands-on, full-time mom. 'With all the children in school all day now, even though Ivo's in Kenya and I'm managing All On

My Own, I just can't justify the expense.'

It is at this point, trust me, that Helen or whoever will cry, as if no one in the history of childcare had ever had such a blinding inspiration before, 'I know! What you need is an au pair!'

Helen is right. But after nine years of sharing the family home with a giddy succession of twenty-two nannies/mothers' helps/au pairs, I know all about au pairs. I have been there, and next week I'm going there again, to the convent in Wimbledon, but I can't pretend my heart's not sinking.

Like us all, I've had a few fabulous Mary Poppinses who still send the children cards on their birthdays and presents at Christmas, whom we can smugly claim are 'part of the family', but many, many more I would cheerfully strangle.

Anyway, my nanny-phobia extends beyond my own house. I'm even more phobic about other people's nannies. I go into a terrible decline if I discover that someone has managed to keep a good one (all my good ones went) for more than nine months, which was my absolute personal best (and I kept her for that long only because I was a first-time mother and told her she didn't have to work in the mornings, babysit, or do any housework).

Other mothers always seemed compelled to confide in me, as I shared my latest nanny crisis (I should explain this was when I worked in an office and had no choice but to hire nannies, lots of them), that they were 'terribly lucky'. I would be told how this other mother had had her Mandy for four years, and now Mandy had her own flat round the corner and Mandy had decided not to be a nursery-school teacher or neurosurgeon after all but, instead, to devote her entire life to looking after this mother's children, because she was 'like, so involved with the kids now' or 'couldn't bear to leave the baby'. Generally, I'd find it helpful, during the course of this gruesome smug-a-thon, to put my hands over my ears and shout: 'I'm not listening! I'm not lis-te-ning!' or pretend to cast around for a blunt object.

So, while my burn rate with nannies is legendary,

everyone else, of course, seems to have the magic touch with help. My sister-in-law, for example, has managed to keep the same nanny for eleven years, and I have often told her that her achievements as a top barrister and mother of four enchanting, well-mannered children pale in comparison.

The strange thing is, now that I now longer have nannies but am going for the au pair option imminently, I feel I've crossed the floor. I'm on the side of nannies, now. I mean, have you ever listened to a mother who has decided – after weeks of kvetching to their girlfriends – to give their nanny the boot? It freezes the blood in your veins.

I have known mothers to sack nannies for losing their house keys ('And you simply won't believe what she did yesterday,' you will hear them screech down their mobiles righteously). For leaving a baby alone for two minutes while they whiz to the loo or for making just one phone call or sitting Junior in front of *The Fimbles* during their 'working hours'.

And I also know a charming couple who went

away just before Christmas, leaving their au pair (remember, they earn a thumping £40 'pocket money' a week) house and dog-sitting what the family had been assured by the dog pound was a three-month-old, spayed rescue puppy.

On Christmas Eve, the family pet made a whelping pen of the father's study and festively produced a mega-litter of ten puppies.

Rather than lounge about the house with her boyfriend, as she had planned, watching DVDs and drinking their way through the wine cellar as any self-respecting au pair would have done, the poor lamb had to spend a merry Christmas knee-deep in soiled newspaper with a hanky over her nose, holding the fort, until the family returned from their three weeks in the Caribbean.

I heard this story from the father so I know it's true. 'And the new puppies weren't as much fun as I've made them sound,' the father admitted to me. But he was still whingeing about the fact that the 'wretched girl' handed in her notice just three days after their return from St Barts.

January

Coco

I'm afraid I've cracked. Despite being diagnosed by Helen with trendy nanny-phobia, I've given in. I admit it. I need help.

It was a bit like my first labour, when I was led to believe in my Notting Hill yoga classes and by the NCT sisterhood (you know, the natural-childbirth Nazis) that I could duke it out on my own without drugs. I was led to believe that, with the right birth partner, massage with essential oils and the most modern, up-to-date essential equipment (er, such as a new Damask nightie, some whale music and a glucose power-bar or two), I too could have an earth-mothery, drug-free, painless delivery. Hah!

After thirty-six hours of what the Americans delicately call 'backache labour' (no, don't let's go there), I was screaming for anaesthesia and if the midwife had only handed me a gun I would have shot myself without hesitation.

So it is with nannies and au pairs. I have been managing without since long before Christmas, as you know. But this week I have had to deal with a feverish, sleepless six-year-old with a hacking cough, and a fracture clinic, and, I remind you with a catch in my voice, no husband.

Fracture clinic. Have you noticed that at the mere mention of those words a vicious one-upmanship erupts between mothers as to whose child has, or has recently had, the worst injury? Ludo had only, unfortunately, a possible broken thumb. Which meant, of course, that the first friend I told about Ludo's little accident stole my thunder completely. She, of course, was 'absolutely shattered' because she had spent the previous night on a camp-bed in hospital with her son while his arm was being 're-set under a general anaesthetic'. And the second friend's son had broken his elbow 'in three places'. See what I mean?

Anyway, it was my crying need for the blessed

epidural of childcare that finally found me driving to Wimbledon, to the Latin-American convent I mentioned, to choose my new au pair.

This place is fantastic – incredible, even – in that, unlike other au pair agencies, you actually get to meet in the flesh (rather than by letter with a black smear where the photo should be) and actually *choose* the person with whom you will share your home, children and husband (only kidding!) for the next few months.

So I prepared our 'nanny bedroom' upstairs, which by rights should be my study but there we go, and off the sickly Oliver and I set. We pulled into the driveway of the convent ten minutes early. By the turning circle there was a white plaster-of-Paris statue of Jesus with a bird on his wrist. I rang the buzzer of the big, redbrick villa and stepped into a darkened hallway.

As my eyes adjusted to the gloom, I realized that about nine dark girls with hair scraped back and vermilion lips were draped in readiness for my arrival on the stairs. As I entered, their Spanish gabble subsided. They chorused '*Hola*' and giggled, then stared at us, with lustrous dark eyes.

I stared back at them. How on earth could you tell? As I examined each one, assessing her for attractiveness, smileyness, slimness and so on, I had this slightly shaming feeling that, in mummy terms, this was not so much like a convent in SW19 as it was the best lil' whorehouse in Texas.

I turned for help to Sister Rosario, who was standing (think Robert Palmer in black habit and wimple in the 'Addicted To Love' video) in front of her dark, exotic charges. She ushered me into her office and I sat, gazed at the portrait of the Virgin, folded my hands demurely and assumed a soulful countenance. 'Tell me which one I should pick,' I begged.

'You do not want . . .' she began, as she studied my face. 'Not Cynthia. I think . . . the best for you is . . . Barbara.'

'And she *is* Catholic?' I heard myself asking, in a pious voice. 'It's a bit like an au pair driving – a bonus, but not essential.'

The nun's face creased with delight. All her girls

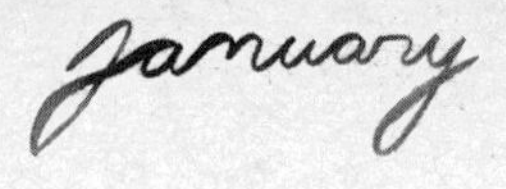

were Catholic, she reassured me. And then she told me about Barbara. Barbara is thirty, from Colombia, single, non-smoking and a qualified paediatrician.

'I'll take her,' I said. 'Wrap her up.'

So I am, as you can imagine, in a state of grace. Any minute now, thanks in part to my cunning revelation that I was baptized a Catholic, Barbara is about to arrive in a taxi to take up residence *chez nous*.

And in our communal garden in Notting Hill I finally have something to boast about. All my neighbours may be mighty merchant bankers and successful novelists and world-famous architects. But we have a doctor in the house. If my friends are going to start taking advantage, as friends do, I think I will have to charge. Premium rates, too.

Weekends, eh. Though the new au pair, Barbara, is so far doing fine (touch wood, ha ha – she's only the twenty-third female to occupy this coveted position to date!), I can't say I get that Friday feeling when I contemplate single-mothering three children, especially as we've already seen both Harry Potter movies and been to the Science Museum and there is now therefore officially nothing left to do, ever.

Still, it's not often that I'm invited to stay somewhere, with the children and minus the husband. So, after Harry Potter last Saturday, we set off for Charing Cross station to catch the 8.30 p.m. to Canterbury, to stay with my sainted sister-in-law Caroline in her small but perfectly formed cottage in Kent.

I have always been proud of how light I travel. When we go to Somerset, I only ever take a washbag, while my husband's stuff fills two entire boots (he insists two cars are necessary for 'flexibility', or, as I put it, 'the freedom to play golf').

This weekend, I was even more economical. Minimal, I should say. I had a small backpack in which I put children's pyjamas, underwear, what M & S call 'toiletries' and Saturday night's supper, because my sister-in-law has many, many fine qualities but Nigella she ain't. I knew that on my return, on Sunday, I would also have Coco, our puppy, so I was even more minimally minded, deciding that the children could wear their Saturday clothes all weekend and that their Gap hoodies would serve as coats if we went for walks, so long as it didn't rain.

On Sunday morning, Caroline very nobly got up first, and by the time I descended I found she had already very kindly served the children a delicious breakfast of marinated artichokes and some Libby's Orange Drink that had been sitting in the fridge since 1996. I found them sitting in a state of slight shock (poss. Coco-Pops withdrawal symptoms?) in front of a snowy screen. It was emitting a headachey noise. 'Put on a video,' I begged, eyeing the Sunday papers. But not even the combined technical expertise of three small children could get the video to work. It was only 8 a.m. We were alone in a small cottage in the rain on Sunday with a broken aerial. We were doomed.

'I know,' I said, trying to hide my panic. 'Let's go to the beach and we'll have a walk, then we'll have lunch somewhere.' Caroline's face lit up (like all her siblings, she loves nothing more than a long expedition, preferably involving stately homes, English antique furniture and many hours of driving). She began taking sinister, reeking paper packages out of the fridge 'just in case the children want a picnic'. We piled into the car. The smell of wet dog and cheese rind filled our nostrils. It was 8.30 a.m.

We aquaplaned around the Kentish weald for some time, then passed a little signpost. 'I know,' said Caroline. 'Let's go and call on my friends the So-and-Sos.' As we were uninvited, and it was 9 a.m. on Sunday morning, we decided it would be best to resist any polite attempts to persuade us across the threshold. Instead, we would cunningly suggest that we took their children on our irresistible rainy-walk-and-scrummy-picnic plan, and then see what came up.

We drove up. The mother came out, we had a nice chat, but she declined our suggestion about taking her children off her hands, murmuring something about people to lunch. Just as we were safely pouring ourselves back into the steamy car, she asked charmingly, 'Are you really sure you don't want a cup of coffee before you go?' We declined (horribly conscious, as two single women with a surfeit of children, of our place in the social food chain), and skated off to St Margaret's-at-Cliffe.

When we got there, we parked by the obelisk memorial to the Dover Patrol, facing the sea. It was raining hard, so we ate the picnic. It was 11 a.m. If you put the windscreen wipers on, you could see that, in France, it was sunny. I took Coco for a walk. When I got back, absolutely soaked, Oliver had spilt his apple juice all over Milly's jeans, and she was sitting in her pants.

I had brought all our stuff with me, so I got the clothes out of the back and Milly put on her pyjama bottoms, which were, I remind you, all she had. We drove to the station and caught the train to London.

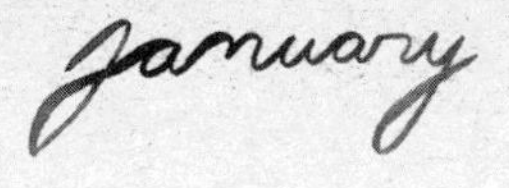

When we got to Cannon Street, we walked out into the street for a taxi.

The boys were covered in mud. Milly was covered in mud and wearing pyjama bottoms. I had the puppy on a length of string because I'd left her lead in the car. It was still raining in London, so we were all soaked through, and minus our outergarments.

No taxis stopped for us, and I think one cabbie even flicked off his light when he saw me jumping about and waving my arms by the side of the road to flag him down.

I can't imagine why.

february

february

I've never felt so important in my life.

At a party, the head of a publishing group was hanging on my every word, while the pixie-ish deputy editor of a national newspaper hovered to speak to me next. Back home, my answering machine's flashing with a message from a beauteous presenter, who had asked me – me! – to ring her back, urgently.

Pleased as I was to receive these unaccustomed attentions, I had a pretty good idea why I was suddenly London's Most Wanted Mummy, and it wasn't because I knew the whereabouts of Osama bin Laden, or even a foolproof method to get children to brush their teeth without being asked every single morning and every single bedtime. Nope. I knew something, in London parenting circles, of even greater note.

february

Last year, my daughter had been through the entry ordeal of one of the most academic girls' schools in London, and all their daughters were about to do the same.

'You must tell me everything,' commanded the publisher. 'What does she need to know for the test? Which times tables? What does she have to have read?'

'And what should she wear to the interviews?' the journalist interrupted, before I could answer the first set of questions.

'Her own clothes, which will reflect her individuality, or do you think her school uniform would be more appropriate?'

I fully understood their concerns. The competition between parents to secure for their offspring places at the best London schools, state *and* independent, starts at conception, and parents will stop at nothing to secure an advantage, however slight, over each other.

One very sensible headmistress I know well, whose own lovely nursery is so oversubscribed she has to turn away even the utterly adorable children of leading Notting Hill celebrities, says she is increasingly putting the letters VVPP on application forms.

'They ring up and mention the films they've directed or that they've been in New York selling the rights to their bestseller,' she confided. 'I put Very, Very Pushy Parent by their child's name.'

My friend Char, mother of three boys, called to register her month-old son at Wetherby in Kensington, the prep school once attended by Harry and Wills. She congratulated herself on being so fast off the blocks, prep-school wise, as she dialled the number. At least she was on top of the 'school situation', as her husband called it, she told herself.

'You're far, far too late,' the registrar barked, when she asked to register her newborn scrap. 'It's absolutely out of the question!'

Char then asked, in her most ringing upper-class tones, how could she be too late for Wetherby when her son was only four weeks old. The registrar sighed and explained that the list for her newborn's year was already full (the VVV Pushiest Parents register foetuses, not babies). And then she sighed again, and asked where Char's father had been at school. 'My father?' repeated Charlotte faintly, in a post-partum haze. 'Um – Eton.' And her husband?

'Also Eton,' said Charlotte. The registration form, needless to say, arrived the next day.

But I mustn't leave you in suspense. What did I tell the anxious fellow mothers whose daughters were about to sit the entrance tests? What tricks of the pushy-mother trade did I exclusively reveal?

'Make sure she knows how to tell the time, knows her six and seven times tables, has read a book like *The Secret Garden*, and doesn't mention the devil-woman, Jacqueline Wilson,' I instructed them, as if imparting the last secrets of Fatima.

'The main thing to remember is that schools expect applicants to have reached a level –' I paused here for dramatic effect – 'two years above their chronological age.'

As my fellow mothers waited avidly for more nuggets, I tried to remember what I could of the morning at the prep school. When I'd reclaimed my daughter after her three hours of tests, I'd grilled her as to what, exactly, she'd had to do.

'We did numbers and then we did clocks and then we had hot chocolate,' she'd said. And? What else? I'd asked, in an ecstasy of maternal anxiety.

'And then we had a biscuit,' she'd finally remembered. 'Oh yes . . .' she trailed off.

'What? What?' I'd almost screamed.

Then she told me she'd been given sheets of newspaper, Sellotape and paperclips and told to make clogs. It had always puzzled me, but still.

These mothers were desperate.

'The other girls were all wearing knee-length kilts, Alice bands and had shirts with piecrust collars,' I told the journalist. 'It was go as square as you dare.' And then I delivered my *pièce de résistance*.

'Make sure you lay in supplies of newspapers, Sellotape and paperclips so you can practise making clogs with her,' I said.

'Clogs?' she said, wonderingly.

'Clogs,' I affirmed.

PS Well, it was a shoo-in for Blanche, Ayesha and Matilda. All thanks to me, of course.

Sometimes, though, things are beyond parental control. You can get your daughters into the fanciest schools in the land, but just try getting them to say please or thank you.

Some friends of ours had another London family to stay in their country house a while back. The guests had two boys, both somewhat younger than the daughters of the house. So Alice laid on the works – scrummy food, riding, screen-based entertainment – to entertain her young male visitors.

The departing family all signed the visitors' book (it was a visitors' book sort of house). As Alice was tidying up, feeling satisfied that the visit of her dear friends had gone so well, her eye lingered over the tome, and she flicked to the entries inscribed by her most recent guests, ink still wet. The parents had written only their names and a scrawled address, on the grounds that it is vulgar to add a comment, but the younger son was moved to add a personal reflection of his own.

'Crap weekend,' his entry ran.

When I heard this story, I was cheered, as I always am when other people's children behave badly. It sort of blunts the despair one feels about one's own children's unmannerly behaviour. Mine, for some reason, have all taken to eating with their fingers since their father has been away.

'Stop dabbling!' I snap. 'It's disgusting! Stop it!' 'But it's finger food,' Milly replies, as she pops another gobbet into her mouth. 'Fruit salad is not finger food,' I correct her. 'When I was your age [children's eyes roll] my grandmother made us eat crisps with a knife and fork [stagey yawns], so I should know.'

Oliver has also taken to asking for cups of tea while

I'm in the middle of doing something. If more than a few seconds goes by and I haven't bustled up with a steaming cuppa like a Lyons nippy, he simply shouts from wherever he is: 'I ordered some tea!' Or, 'Mother, I need my tea,' like some coal-blacked miner, home from t'pit.

And oh, how I secretly relish it when other people's children fail to thank/say please/look one in the eye when saying goodbye, the basic courtesies every parent tries to instil in their offspring. 'Can I have the potatoes,' ordered one child who came to Sunday lunch last week. I sat there grimly and waited, without passing the potatoes.

'Do you perhaps mean "May I have the potatoes, please,"?' I enunciated, showing my gums, in front of the child's German mother, who beamed with joy as her son helped himself to several Kartoffeln.

Then I found myself asking over pudding, somewhat pointedly, 'Are you very strong on manners in Germany?' '*Nein*, we are very relaxed type of parents,' she said, then yodelled in German to her children the relative merits of my apple crumble (homemade) versus the (obviously more lovely and shop-bought) sticky toffee pudding.

And oh, the pleasure it gives to meet and greet children and hear the same old excuses I've made on behalf of my children being repeated back to me.

'It's because he's not on his *home ground*,' a visiting mother confided to me, as her eight-year-old shrieked over some trifling incident. 'She's just exhausted, aren't you, darling?' was the next offering, over a ghastly suppertime. And then my favourite, which came at the moment when one traditionally grips a child by the shoulders and frogmarches her up to the hostess to 'say goodbye nicely'. (She refused.) Yes, out came the old 'She's only like this when I'm around, of course – when I'm not here she's incredibly well behaved, I'm told.'

It's easy enough to convey the black and white of basic manners, please and thank you. But how to convey – without a snobbish disquisition – the chiaroscuro of etiquette? That you don't say,

'Thank you for the meal,' 'Can I use your toilet?' or, 'No thanks, I'm full'?

Two years ago, we were staying in Sicily, and were expected to labour, before leaving, over the pigskin-bound visitors' book (in France and Italy, to give long panegyrics is customary). We composed our frilly tributes. My daughter, then aged seven, grabbed the exquisite tome and settled on the loggia to leave her mark. My husband and I were quietly confident (we regard her as rather artistic) that she would leave one of her graceful, childish sketches.

We were halfway to Catania before our Sicilian hosts would have had an opportunity to look at the *livre d'or*, where they would have seen that our insincere gushes had benefited from a lively addition: a Biro drawing of Pikachu the Pokémon, which took up an entire vellum page, and had been carefully coloured in with her neon-yellow highlighter pen.

'Crap weekend' would, I suspect, have been a more welcome inscription.

february

I've never felt so squashed in my life. After my triumph in getting all my friends' children into schools, and I've been sacked. In the middle of the school year, too, when I'm flying solo.

Yes, I am – for the moment, anyway – no longer welcome on my Notting Hill-to-Hampstead school run.

Last week, I confess, I didn't take Child A to his front door. M'lud, I allowed a strapping nine-year-old to walk, unaccompanied, 50 yards to his home and ring his own doorbell, as I drove off.

It was wrong, wrong, wrong and I will never do it again. In my defence, this is my first school run, nobody told me the rules, and I certainly never expected Child A to snitch on me!

'This is Child A's mother,' snapped the American voice on my answering machine (parents of other children only ever identify themselves by their child's first name).

'I'm ringing to say that I'm really upset and really surprised, frankly, that you didn't escort Child A to our front door and wait to see whether there was a responsible adult there to receive him within. Please call me back at the law firm so we can discuss your behaviour.' When I called back, she sacked me. 'Look, I really believe in car pooling, but this isn't working,' she said. 'Don't bother to pick him up next week.'

Which meant, of course, that I would have to schlep up to the boys' school on the day *her* nanny usually fetched *my* son.

Clearly, I needed to brief myself a bit better, and to learn the School Run Rules, if life was going to be worth living. So I asked my neighbour, who is such a dedicated car pooler that when her son got into Colet Court, one of the smartest boys' prep schools in London, she traded in her silver Porsche for a Chrysler Grand Voyager in a racy navy blue.

What she said is that, apart from the obvious stuff about seatbelts, punctuality and so on, mummies or parents'n'carers on school runs must:

1) Carry mobiles at all times, have the other school-run mummies' numbers programmed to memory, and attend a pre-termly coffee morning to work out the rota and double check telephone numbers.
2) At morning pick-up, ring once or knock lightly at the door, and not just sit in the car.
3) At p.m. drop-off, observe the dietary requirements of the children she is driving.
4) Make sure that children are inside their front doors with an adult before driving off.

As you can imagine, I listened to this list with cheeks aflame. It was now clear, as if I needed to be told again, that I was unfit for what Child A's mother called 'car pooling'. My friend then said that if one mother broke any single one of these rules, just once, the other mothers met in camera at Starbucks in Holland Park to decide her punishment.

'There was this one mother who would never ring the doorbell at pick-up.' She frowned at the memory.

'She honked, at 7 a.m. We told her not to honk, very nicely, of course, but she had to go.'

'Go?'

'Yes, it was very embarrassing because we see her every day, at the school, and the children are friends. But we had to drop her from the run. We had no choice.'

She then went on to explain it was not done to bring chocolate (blood-sugar swings), or indeed any other carbohydrate, as 'snack'.

Only peeled fruit, gluten-free cookies, pulses, grains and so on were permitted by London School Run Rules.

It was at that point that I remembered, with horror, that every time I'd driven Child A home, I'd bought him a Snickers – the ultimate calorie bomb, with a payload not just of fat grammes and dairy products but also peanuts, which as we know can kill without warning at any time. To think what had happened to the other mother – sacked for honking – what on earth would the attorney do to me if she ever found out?

I think I'd better quickly call Child A's mom to ask for one further offence to be taken into consideration – and just pray for a suspended sentence and a rapid return to the car-pooling community.

My campaign against over-parenting (you know, not allowing your eight-year-old to walk 50 yards alone to their own front door, installing nanny cams, supervising children even in their own bedrooms, and so on) suffered a minor reverse last week. It was Saturday morning. The children were raptly watching commercials for tooth-rotting drinks and sugar-laden cereals in the playroom, as is their wont. I wanted to catch the post. As Barbara was asleep upstairs, I subjected the situation to what I call my Home Alone test, which is: could my actions lead to an unfortunate newspaper headline? Having judged that 'Mum

Abandons Telly Tots to Post Letter' wasn't a story, I nipped out. But, when I returned to the scene, there were not three children sitting in front of Ant and Dec. There were only two, and I simply knew in my bones that my youngest – my baby! – was not in the house.

'Where's Oliver?' I demanded.

'Dunno. Went upstairs, I think,' one of the others answered, without looking up. I quickly searched the house.

Then I did a fingertip search, which involved repeatedly screaming the six-year-old's name, turning out laundry baskets, peering under beds, and hunting in the garden. After he had been missing for thirty-five minutes, I went out into the street to see if he had followed me out to the postbox. A neighbour was passing, latte in hand. 'Hi,' I hailed her, trying to appear calm. 'Have you seen Oliver?' I should remind you that it was Saturday, midmorning, and I live near Ladbroke Grove.

The Portobello Market is so close that I spend my entire time what I call 'marketing', i.e., going to and fro from the Portobello to buy a few apples.

The whole area was teeming with tourists, and Japanese with cameras in search of the blue front door to Hugh Grant's flat or the Tlavel Bookshop.

My neighbour gave me a thoughtful look, shook her head and let herself into the house, thus avoiding any involvement in a tiresomely time-consuming missing-child situation.

I ran up and down the street, yelling my son's name, as skinny blondes in very *au courant* peasant blouses and jeans teetered past me on their way to The Cross. Then I saw a police car approaching, slowly, as if looking for someone – a small boy, perhaps! This emboldened me to flag it down, apologize, and explain my child had vanished.

'How old is he?' asked the young man, giving me a look. 'And what is his name?' I stammered out the answers. 'We have a male person answering to your description,' he announced. 'If you would be so kind as to alight into the vehicle, madam,' he continued in fluent police-speak, 'I will convey you to this person's location.'

We went up Ladbroke Grove. We turned right again, and then I saw a fleet of police cars double-parked in Lansdowne Road, blue lights flashing.

A crowd of my neighbours had gathered. But I was oblivious – I had caught sight of the back of my son's white-blond head, and I was past shame.

He was sitting in the driver's seat, being shown how to turn what he still calls the 'nee-naw' lights on and off. I alighted from my vehicle in an ecstasy of relief, and scooped him up.

As the nice policeman took us home, Oliver explained, between sobs, how he had gone on a walk to 'find Mummy'. The policeman kept a manly silence, but I, too, was weeping.

Even though we have already been chuckling about Oliver's weekend 'walk', I have not emerged emotionally unscathed from this little escapade. The unintended consequence of my two-minute absence, you see, was that my young son let himself out of the house. And the police car was not looking for Oliver, I belatedly realized, but the adult who was supposed to be in charge of him.

I can't help thinking of that A. A. Milne poem about James James Morrison Morrison Weatherby George Dupree. He was the little boy who touchingly took great care of his mother even though he was only three, and who said: 'You must never go down to the end of the town / If you don't go down with me.' But his mother simply disappeared, having thought she could get down to the end of the town and be back in time for tea – the 1920s equivalent, I suppose, of posting a letter while the children are engrossed in Saturday-morning TV.

Well, I know that many people find A. A. Milne's poetry emetic, so I won't go on. But that particular poem – about the little boy and the mother who was 'lost, stolen or strayed' – can now bring a little tiny tear to this maternal eye.

March

March

I was in the pet shop the other day in Primrose Hill, buying some food for Coco, when I heard a voice by the chewy-toy display.

'My child. My son,' crooned the voice. I did a detour past chewy toys to confirm my suspicions, and was not surprised to find a middle-aged woman cradling a large and rather decrepit poodle in her arms while he licked her on the mouth.

Averting my eyes, and practising the pursed-lipped expression I am going to deploy when I come across my teenage children snogging their unsuitable friends, I paid for my kibble and fled, feeling weak.

When I got home, though, I took my shopping straight down to the kitchen, and Coco came up to me wagging her tail. 'Yeth, baby,' I told her in a high-pitched lisp. 'Oh, yeth, baby! Look what mummy'th got for you. Kibble! And Puppy Pouches with wabbit.'

At least parents are dimly aware that others do not find their children as enchanting as they do, and that it is better, on the whole, not to broadcast their child's special achievements to a captive audience of other parents. But most pet owners are oblivious to such nuances.

My husband and I go around confiding to other dog owners that Coco is, quite possibly, the cleverest and sweetest dog in the world. We also tell long anecdotes to complete strangers (much as I've seen grandparents on buses get out the snaps of their grandchildren) about how Coco (a Lab-collie cross) retrieves sticks, answers to her name, gobbles her dinner in seconds and other unprecedented doggy feats.

But now the household is divided. We all love Coco, of course, and there is no doubt that she is the child substitute the whole family has been longing for. But I want to have her spayed and the others don't.

March

'How can you, of all people, deny a woman,' my husband says, as he sits with Coco on his lap, gazing into her caramel eyes, 'the right to bear children?' It's hard to know where to begin when your husband insists on talking about an animal only in human terms, but we all do it, and that is the least of our worries. He knows, or at least I think he knows, that Coco is a dog. The point is, Coco is to come into season in June and Ernie, the golden Labrador that lives on the other side of the communal garden, already thinks Coco is hot, smokin' hot, and is determined to 'marry' her at whatever cost.

Several times a day, Ernie bursts out of his own garden, comes hurtling across the communal garden like a heat-seeking missile, and hurls himself against our back door. Then he sits like a lovesick swain, giving the occasional howl. I have to drag him bodily by the collar the 500 yards back to his house. Ernie's parents are very responsibly spending a small fortune on Alcatraz-style iron railings to gate the dog, but I can see this is leading to trouble.

March

'Coco's clearly a slut,' says Ernie's mummy, when I bring her dog back. 'Are you quite sure she's not on heat? Ernie's so desperate to get at her that he hurt his leg quite badly when he was breaking down the gate. Isn't there some pill you can give her?'

'Ernie has a one-track mind,' I reply, rather hotly. 'Coco's not on heat, and she certainly isn't leading him on. Ernie is stalking her.'

The trouble is not with Ernie's family. On the contrary. Nicola and I have merely assumed the stereotypes appropriate to the sex of our pets. I am the protective parent, anxious to defend my daughter's maidenly purity, while Nicola adopts a breezy, boys-will-be-boys approach to her unruly pup. The letting rip is all rather good fun and, as we are talking about dogs, rather than children, we have no need to sugar-coat our opinions.

No, the real trouble is knowing – because all the owners of 'intact' dogs have told me so – that, if one of the communal-garden dogs does succeed in marrying Coco, I will be left holding the babies.

March

Ernie is outside the garden door as I write, waiting for Coco to emerge to powder her nose. No doubt when she comes into season all the other testosterone-fuelled dogs will join his stakeout.

I never realized that dog ownership would be quite so complicated. I never expected Coco to have such ardent admirers. Perhaps we should have stuck with something small and safe, like Crumpy, I sometimes wonder. Crumpy is Honeyballs' successor and very much along the same lines (all hamsters, sad or happy, are very much alike in my book – the only thing that distinguishes them is this: is it a live hamster or a dead hamster?).

'I know that the only person who is really interested in my hamster,' my mother observed sadly the other day, 'is me.'

March

On Shrove Tuesday, we held a family discussion (as my husband has now repatriated himself from Kenya) about what to give up for Lent.

Milly announced that she wanted to 'take up' eating salad instead of giving something up, reminding me that my father was for many years convinced that being 'on a diet' meant you ate an orange after every three-course meal.

After animated argument, it was agreed that eating salad on top of her usual healthy intake of comestibles did not amount to a sufficient purification of the flesh, so she has volunteered to give up snacks between meals, too.

Ludo took the same approach as Milly, undertaking to switch from Honey Nut Cheerios to Raisin Wheats throughout Quadragesima. Oliver refused to give up anything, wailing that he was 'not fat', which required a long talk about the meaning of the Lenten fast and the enrichment of human spirit. 'Does this mean we can't have Nutella any more?' he gasped at the end of the sermon, implying that this sacrifice was too great for his frame to bear.

March

My husband undertook to give up smoking (including cigars) and alcohol. I promised to give up chocolate and wine.

That was Shrove Tuesday.

On Ash Wednesday, having half-walked, half-jogged around the Round Pond in Kensington Gardens, I opened the glove compartment in the car to see whether the king-size Mars bar that Oliver nibbled the day before was still there. Just to check, you understand.

After I had verified its existence, I slammed the glove compartment shut, drooling only slightly. I couldn't, I told myself. Not on the first morning of Lent. I knew I had very little self-control, but that would be ridiculous!

I tried switching on the radio and listening to a discussion of IVF on *Woman's Hour*. But it was impossible. Not eating the Mars bar was even harder than taking a chicken, bacon and avocado granary sandwich to eat on a long train journey and not eating it before the train has actually left the station.

And then, your honour, I don't know what exactly happened. It was like a dream. Everything sort of went into slow motion and, the next thing I knew, I was aware of licking the last shreds of caramel from the packet and punishing myself by reading the nutritional-information box, which told me with how many hundreds of calories of sugar and fat I had just bombed my system.

Having failed so totally on the choccy front, I am determined to do better on the drinking and things are going well, if only because I have broadened, one might say, the terms of reference.

Yes, I am following a regime of 'modified Lent', much as most people I know are on a diet called 'modified Atkins'.

With modified Lent, I allow myself to drink only outside the home, just as modified Atkins allows one to eat a lot of meat and a little of everything else.

Modified Lent, I calculate, will also permit me rum punches when I go to Jamaica next week on my fact-finding mission (i.e., luxury freebie). But I still thought I was pretty strong not to crack when I got an excited call from my vintner Jack Scott this week. Before I could stop him and explain that I wasn't drinking at home, he started telling me about a 'very cheeky, very sexy, very fleshy' Bordeaux, with 'a lot of new wood' in it.

'Mmm.' I couldn't help being tempted. 'What are you asking for a case?'

Well, it was jolly reasonable and, after I explained my regime, we agreed to delay the delivery to Good Friday. It's so important to have little treats to look forward to – next week's jaunt to the Caribbean, cheeky wines, etc. – this tricky time of year, I always think.

'What have I done to deserve this?' I moaned as I came to on Monday morning, to the sound of waves breaking decorously on a beach, sand the colour of shortbread below my window. I rose from my kingsize bed and stumbled to the window.

Young men with ebony torsos and clad in red shorts were – I rubbed my jet-lagged eyes – actually combing the sand with long rakes. I can only describe the sea as a turquoise. Across the sparkling bay, rimmed with exuberant tropical vegetation, coconut trees and emerald grass, I could see a low-lying, pale-blue colonial house which I didn't know, then, was the Jamaica Inn.

And all I had to do today, according to our leader, was relax on the beach, acclimatizing. The trip into the hills to 'connect with nature', as he put it, was an option for after lunch.

I don't know about you, but whenever I go anywhere and I am removed from work, family obligations and the demands of running a house, three children and a dog, I become consumed with a whole new set of anxieties. In my case, these centre on the Manichean struggle between idleness and greed on the one hand and healthful and educational activity on the other.

To give you an example: when I was reading classics at university, one summer my father had taken a house about ninety minutes from Rome. I was asked every day whether I wanted to drive into the eternal city. My father would mildly point out that I was taking papers for Finals in art, architecture and ancient history. And I had never seen the Forum or the Colosseum. Or been to Rome.

'No thanks,' I would reply, with some irritation. 'I don't often get the chance to lie by the pool all day sunbathing and reading Jilly Cooper. Maybe tomorrow.'

So, when I heard our itinerary for the week, I naturally had to struggle to suppress feelings of panic. How would I fit in the spa, tennis, aromatherapy and the requisite four hours on the beach sipping fruit punch if we were going to be spending long spells in the minibus, seeing the 'real' Jamaica, throbbingly alive and beautiful as a Bounty ad, pulsating with little shacks selling Red

Stripe and blaring Bob Marley from dawn to dusk?

'I get very sick if I have to spend any length of time in a minibus, particularly on winding roads,' I warned our tour leader, as he outlined a trip into the coffee plantations of the Blue Mountains. 'The last time I was in one I was actually sick on the driver's shoes. I promise.'

So that's idleness. I reckon my greed is even more of an issue. When I sit down to breakfast, I tell myself that I will only have coffee and fruit. But then I can't help seeing that there is French toast with maple syrup or blueberry pancakes, and I become engrossed for long periods.

'Are you OK?' I will be asked solicitously by some chap, who has already ordered his eggs and bacon without a second's thought. 'Yes, yes, I'm just thinking what to have,' I will explain. Women are all too familiar with this dilemma, but I find that it has to be explained to men that, when a woman is looking pensive, it's not, on the whole, because she is thinking about the last days of Socrates. She is more likely to be in deep contemplation of what she's going to have, or has already had, for lunch. Or supper.

Which explains my moan, of course, when I looked out of my window on to paradise my first morning in Jamaica. What had I done to deserve this? And, more to the point, how could I enjoy it when I knew that I had parked all three children with my friend Fiona for the entire week?

So the last issue I have to deal with, in the absence of anything else to do, is guilt. Women are constantly being told to pamper themselves more and to spend time 'on themselves', but there is nothing more anxious-making than self-indulgence. A woman is often never happier than when she is feeling exhausted and put-upon, in my experience. So I've dealt with the guilt by telling myself that this week is even harder on me than it is on Fiona, who is stuck in rainy London looking after my three children (and a dog) while I am in Jamaica and my husband is in Ghana. Though I'm not sure she would accept the logic in that, it's definitely working for me.

March

I can remember it as if it were yesterday. The day my father talked to us openly and honestly, without a trace of embarrassment, about the birds and the bees.

We were sitting on the bench seat in the back of the Opel Kadett on the way back to boarding school. It was Sunday evening and we were returning from a weekend exeat. Rain was beading the windows, and I had that leaden feeling in the pit of my stomach. My father broke the fuggy silence.

'Um,' he began, masterfully. 'Er. Ummm.'

'What?' my elder brother and I grunted in unison.

My father kept his eyes on the yellow headlights stubbing the dark road ahead. We passed the church at Coleman's Hatch, looming through wet shrubbery. My stomach clenched, because this meant that in a second we would be turning up the drive to Ashdown. My father coughed.

'Ahem,' he continued. 'Um, your mother [cough] has asked me to . . .' and he trailed off. Suddenly, aged eleven and twelve, we had a horrible suspicion of the topic he was essaying to raise (my mother had already given us detailed books written by child psychologists to read, but she clearly thought some additional paternal input was required), so we headed him off at the pass.

'Dada, it's under control,' we said. 'Don't worry. We know all about it. It's fine.'

'Fine,' he echoed. 'Hey ho! As long as you don't do it too often! Ha ha.' Then he coughed a couple more times, changed the subject, dropped us back at school and drove off.

I thought about this a lot this week, because, point one, my son is just ten, about the age I was during this full and frank exchange with my father, and point two, when I powered up my laptop last week, after I got back from Jamaica, I spotted this unusual new icon on the desktop: a picture of a movie camera, accompanied by one giveaway word: 'OrgyCam'.

I regret to tell you that I double-clicked on the icon and was presented with a screen split eight ways, so punters could pay premium rates to watch their preference. (I'd rather not go into it, but suffice it to say that the range was catholic in the extreme, left little to the imagination and offered viewing possibilities I did not know existed and prayed my children remained ignorant of as well.)

'What's this doing on my desktop?' I asked my husband accusingly.

'Don't ask me; I haven't touched your computer,' he replied. 'Have you been surfing for porn again, ha ha!'

'Of course I haven't,' I snapped primly. But it haunted me all day. Could one of the children (six, nine and ten) have possibly downloaded it? I searched my memory for when the children had borrowed my laptop, because theirs has been broken almost since the day I bought it.

But all I retrieved from my memory bank was the fact that my daughter had used it to work on her project on Tudor fashion, mainly about kirtles and ruffs. And my eldest son, I now remembered, had asked me if he could download a CD from school on to my laptop. It was called *Around the Bible in 40 Days*. How racy is that?

I have to say, the whole business has made me feel wretched. I even at one point called ChildLine. The people there were brilliant and said to tell my two older children that, whatever it was, I wouldn't be upset, but we needed to talk to them about surfing the Net 'For Their Own Safety'.

I then rang a friend and told her about my horrifying discovery and she laughed.

'Everyone has one experience like that with their computers and their children and then gets some parental-control software,' she says. 'Mine was when my mother-in-law rang up about one night we'd all been staying with her and she was out playing bridge. The phone bill came in with an entry for that night for £50, charged to a premium-rate number. I paid up, challenged my eldest son and he absolutely denied it. But the awful truth is I reckon he'd been logged on to some hardcore site for two hours.'

My children have no idea how it got there. It came in overnight. A virus. I've got parental controls now (on the computer, at any rate). But isn't it peculiar? In my day, parents embarrassed children by telling them, in a beardie way, about the joy of sex. Now, it's my children on the Web who reduce me to a jelly of discomfort and fear.

April

April

As two of my brothers live there and it is springtime, I rather thought a long weekend in Paris. I would treat myself to a City Break. I would go with my mother, who also rather thought Paris at this time of year: shop, stroll along the Seine, look up old boyfriends and buzz about the bars of Pigalle on the back of little brother Jo's new red Vespa.

'My mother needs to go to Paris and can't manage her bags on the Eurostar,' I said, assuming a pious, daughterly expression. 'I propose I go with her to help, stay over Saturday night and be back on Sunday to help with homework.'

'I think it's a great idea,' my husband responded, agreeably. 'On one condition,' he added. 'You take Oliver.'

I have to hand it to him. If there is a more

effective barrier to girlie shopping, late soirées and lingering over espressos than my six-year-old son, I have yet to hear of it. Insisting I take him as chaperone was, I acknowledged as I sat on the Eurostar with a bagful of story-tapes, sweets, GameBoy and a micro-scooter, a stroke of genius.

The weekend was lovely, actually, even if it was a full-time job for five adults (my mother, two brothers and I, plus one sister-in-law) just keeping my son entertained. I know I can't be the only parent to have noticed this, but why is it that one child on his own expands to fill the void created by the absence of siblings? On Friday, we took Oliver to the Tuileries to watch the boules. On Saturday morning, we took him to the Luxembourg Gardens, where he was enchanted by the antique carousel, where the children sitting on mounts in the outer ring clutch pointed wooden sticks.

As the carousel spins, they sit like medieval jousters, lances held at the horizontal, and try to spear their sticks through metal rings extruded, one after another, from a sausage-like contraption. At the end of the ride, the children proudly hold aloft their batons, and count off how many rings they have captured. This was such a successful expedition that on Saturday afternoon we could think of nothing more entertaining than to go back and cheer Oliver on as he tried to spear some rings all over again, so that's what we did.

As I had promised to be back at lunchtime on Sunday, we hurried to the Gare du Nord soon after breakfast and boarded the train to London. Now, I don't know about you, but if I have to travel soon after waking up, I feel a bit queasy. There was an awful time in Syria last year when we were touring Crusader castles, and I got on the minibus shortly after breakfast and sat, head spinning and stomach churning, as we twisted our way up to the Krak des Chevaliers.

On arrival, the others went off to admire the vaulted passages and portcullis, but I lay supine on the back seat of the darkened minibus, praying for the end to come quickly. At length our little party – including my then editor, Brigid, and an expert on the Mamelukes and his Turkish wife – came trickling back to the van, with expressions of concern. They settled into their seats with murmurs of 'poor you' and 'such a shame to miss the glacis . . . and the machicolations were exceptional!' I moved wanly to the front, and sat next to our Syrian guide.

The doors glided shut. The driver turned the ignition. I apparently gave a little cry of 'Bag!' and neatly vomited all over the guide's shoes. 'So typical of you,' my husband said sympathetically, later. 'You have to be the centre of attention at all times, even if that means being sick inside a stationary vehicle in full view of everyone.'

As soon as the train left Paris, I settled Oliver with a tape, opened the paper and was soon engrossed in a harrowing account of conditions inside the prisons in Iraq.

I began to feel somewhat poorly. I tried leaning my head against the window and closing my eyes, but it was no good. Oliver was angelic. 'Have a little rest, Mummy,' he kept saying, quiet as a mouse.

April

Even when I got into bed that night back in London, I felt drained and nauseous. Maybe after my 'weekend off' I shouldn't have given that little moan as I lay down in bed, and muttered about 'still feeling train-sick', but I couldn't help it.

'How can you still be "train-sick" eight hours after disembarking?' my husband asked, flumping his pillow in irritation. 'So typical of you, when there's a war on and people dying every day in Iraq,' he continued, 'to find conditions on board the Eurostar intolerable.'

Coco attained a 'significant milestone' in her development last week. It was her first birthday. My daughter, whose vocation is organization, naturally started laying in Coco's presents ages ago. So on the big day Coco received the following haul: a dog-bowl made of transparent acetate with dog biscuits inset in the rim.

Next, a dog-basket from Cath Kidston in hot pink with a blowsy rose print. 'The fabric fades beautifully when machine-washed,' says the label, and I have to confess that this shabby-chic little detail closed the sale. Then there were stocking-fillers – a microfibre blanket and a diamante-studded collar that sets off her gleaming, sooty coat to perfection.

I thought that took care of Coco's birthday. My daughter had other ideas. She had a plan. She is the Lady Elizabeth Anson of party-planning.

A few days before the great event, I came into the kitchen to find Bettina, Flora and Rosie with Milly. They were stuffing envelopes like some committee of Tory ladies, only much more purposeful. 'What's going on, guys? Can I see?' I asked, in my most cringingly hearty voice.

Milly handed me a card. 'Puppy Party!' it said in purple felt-tip, beside paw-prints and little drawings of Coco. Inside, it spelt out the name of the invitee, date, time and list of activities. It was then that I started experiencing all the symptoms of a panic attack.

My daughter takes anniversaries very seriously, hates to leave any event in the sentimental calendar unmarked (I received four beautiful handmade Mother's Day presents), and is already planning her big, white wedding right down to the grosgrain ribbons on the bridesmaids' slippers.

'Puppy Treat Hunt! – Pass the Pawcel! – Dog Races! – Birthday Tea!' it said. Five of Coco's best friends had been invited: Jack, her ardent suitor Ernie, George, Barley and Ginkgo. 'What super fun!' I bleated, looking down at their shining faces. I knew that resistance would be futile.

The longed-for day arrived. Having managed to persuade Milly that I was not going to spend an entire day making a Jane Asher-style bone-shaped cake with royal icing, there was no way I could avoid a trip to Portobello Pets to buy, as she put it, 'all the stuff' for the party.

We had already wrapped a pouch of Pedigree

Chum in paper for the Pass the Pawcel stage of festivities, and so my main outlay was on treats and chews for the Puppy Treat Hunt (which we imagined as a sort of Easter Egg Hunt, only with less wailing that Child A had found all the eggs) and the Doggy Bags. When we got home, Milly made up the Doggy Bags, filling each with a rawhide bone, a Beggin' Strip and biscuits, for each pup to take home.

At the appointed hour of 4 p.m., we went out into the communal garden. Ernie was already there, and gave Coco a squeaky toy. The next arrival was George, a dachshund, who gave Coco a squeaky toy too. As the races got under way Ginkgo and Barley (Lab and Retriever) arrived. Barley was victor ludorum. The only no-show was a terrier, Jack.

The Treat Hunt served as the perfect ice-breaker, and soon all the dogs were tearing round the garden in a pack, with Ernie trying to mount the birthday girl at every opportunity.

Coco's birthday has indeed been a milestone. It made my daughter see that it is more fun watching someone you love have fun than trying to have fun yourself. But the puppy party could, I fear, make me unpopular among my fellow Notting Hill mummies.

It is not enough, now, to give each of your children a proper party on their birthday every year, and/or send them into school with a tray of homebaked goodies. Did you think you could get off so lightly? You have to throw one for the dog too!

At Coco's party, everyone came on time, some with generous gifts. Nobody insulted anyone or burst into tears, and the total budget (drinks included) was £4.80.

Frankly, it was the most successful social event I have ever hosted.

I think it all started at the weekend, when we went down to Exmoor, and the stag hunt came through our yard. Suddenly, a pack of hounds was swarming about us, sniffing our trousers with interest, cocking their legs hither and yon. Then came the cry of a horn in the copse above the duck pond. The master gave an answering toot, called to the hounds, wheeled about on his mare and they all poured importantly up the lane, yapping, leaving behind a number of steaming packets and the rank scent of kennels.

Poor Coco simply didn't know what to do with herself. At first, she tried showing them who was king of the castle by jumping on a wall and barking. Then she went inside and curled up on a chair, with a defeated look in her eyes.

It was a bit like during Crufts, as I remember. Coco didn't seem to mind the 'toy' and 'utility' groups so much, because she could see us all giggling and pointing at the bouffant up-dos that take their besotted owners six hours' grooming to perfect. I like to imagine Coco regarded these lapdogs much as a busy working barrister and mother of four children in state school, say, would regard a Knightsbridge trophy wife.

But as a Labrador-collie cross – two of the most hard-working, intelligent and diligent breeds – she did have some inevitable feelings of inferiority with the working and gun dogs. Then she could see without any doubt that not all dogs were merely loved and cosseted and cared for, spending much of the day snoozing by the Aga. She could see that some dogs play a serious role in life. So it has become more than clear to Coco, aged one, that she is not Having It All. She is, in a very real sense, unfulfilled.

Of course, she has a loving home and walkies, scrummy din-dins and a dog-basket (from Cath Kidston, I remind you) called 'Beddy-bies', but she doesn't have either of the two things that tend to make life complete for any bitch, which are, of course, babies and a career.

I didn't fully understand the extent to which dogs suffer the same identity crises as their mistresses when I had her spayed, against my husband's wishes, the other day (I have hardly dared mention it – emotions have been running very high). But I did it. And when I picked her up from the vet, she was whimpering and shuddering and I knew I was in terrible trouble.

'It's the cruellest thing anybody has ever done to anyone,' raged my husband, after informing me that he had wept twice since he heard the news.

'I can't believe that you, of all people,' he continued in a shaking voice, 'could deprive another woman of the right to bear children.' (That's what he always says.) The awful thing is, I am now beginning to feel that I was wrong, after all, to have had Coco spayed before she even had one litter. Bear in mind that this wrong feeling comes from someone – me – who follows the Blair doctrine on Iraq ('I was right then and I am right now' and 'It's not my fault') on almost everything.

Spaying would have been more acceptable, I now see, if Coco was a working dog, but Coco is not, so she has the possibility of neither a career, as it were, nor babies. The poor girl cannot honestly claim to be 'juggling' anything. And her existential sense of pointlessness has been heightened by the children's discovery of a television show from America called *Dogs with Jobs*.

The children sit rapt as heroic police dogs search for bombs and drugs and arsonists . . . as military working dogs are filmed casing the joints . . . or as service dogs showcase their skills in pulling wheelchairs, opening doors, or dialling 911.

Now, I realize that I could always give Coco counselling, but I don't feel it's necessary, even if I can imagine her muttering that she's 'just a pet' when the hounds enter the yard, in just the same way that I've heard women saying 'just a mum' to men at dinner parties.

The truth is that Coco is, in fact, working overtime as my 'therapy dog' (popular in rehab centres over the pond, I have learnt). After all, she always wags her tail when she sees me, never allows some minor unpleasantness to sour our friendship, and finds my cooking lip-smackingly delicious. An unblemished record of appreciation that most human 'best friends' cannot hope to match.

april

coco

Sometimes, I have to confess, I often half-hope that someone will at some point look at me, shake their head in admiration, and sigh, 'I don't know how she does it.' No one has yet, but in readiness for the moment I have decided to write down the timetable of my average school day. In case someone does ask.

We get up at 6.45 a.m., and get two boys fed and into their father's car by 7.40 a.m. I leave the house at 8 a.m., on foot with my daughter and Coco, drop Milly at school, walk the dog, am home again by 9.40 a.m. to check emails and do a spot of work; then I wander out for a sandwich, come home, go to Sainsbury's, return from Sainsbury's, unload the Sainsbury's, unpack the Sainsbury's, and then hop back in the car to pick up the children.

It's dull, isn't it? Anyway, since I've started, I might as well finish. Fast forward to 5 p.m., by which time all after-school clubs have wound up (and, since you ask, son No. 1 does drama and history clubs and plays the trumpet, son No. 2 does chess and violin, and my daughter does choir, piano, gymnastics, chess and an art class). We take, as you can see, a studiously minimal approach to extracurricular activities in our household. I hate it when I see all these scary London hyper-parents over-scheduling their children, don't you? By 5ish I'm usually back home again.

Then I make the children's supper, which I try to have them eat before 6 p.m., when, following a short but sickeningly violent disagreement over whose turn it is to lie on the new squishy chocolate-suede beanbag, they watch *The Simpsons*.

After *The Simpsons*, we have a 6.30 p.m. homework session, which is something of a recent innovation in our house (as is, if I'm being honest, any set times for anything, but things were getting so chaotic that we are trialling this radical new supper-television-homework-bedtime routine thing).

So I invite you to leave the timetable of events I have so far chronicled to picture this homely, orderly scene: the kitchen table is covered with dirty dishes, schoolbags are strewn across the floor, Coco is licking the smeared cutlery in the dishwasher, and I rise from the supper table, clap my hands together (this handclap is my weedy-liberal version of the imperious von Trapp whistle) and say, in a bright voice: 'Right, guys! It's homework time! Settle down at the big table and, when I've finished clearing up, I'll join you . . .' Then the telephone rings and, as I go to answer it, the children seize the moment to sneak upstairs to play *Medieval Total War Viking Invasion* on the computer. (No wonder soldiers call enemy fire 'incoming'. Incoming calls shatter the fragile truce of early evening quicker than a mortar.)

'Listen,' I pant down the telephone to a mother who has rung to see whether son No. 1 will be free to come to the Science Museum on the Wednesday of half-term at 2.45 p.m., still four weeks hence, 'that sounds lovely, but can we talk about it nearer the time?' Then I shout up to the children, 'Guys, come down', in a voice that starts sounding reasonable and assertive, but always ends bonkersly in a shriek: 'Or it'll be *Medieval Total Spanking*!'

There is silence. Then I hear an altercation start about whose turn it is to attack the nunnery at Lindisfarne and – wheeee! – there's incoming again.

'Is this a bad time?' demands the caller, somewhat crossly. 'There never seems to be a good time to ring.'

You see? It's absolutely hopeless. But I suppose I could always let the machine pick up calls, something I am loath to do because, if I'm being honest, I quite like being phoned and secretly welcome distractions from Motherhood, the Most Important Job in the World. My friend Tessa takes the job very seriously, though. So this is how she deals with incoming calls.

'Tessa and Francis are not able to take your call at the moment,' callers are told. 'But if you are calling between 5 and 8 p.m., you will have to leave a message. Because Tessa will be occupied with the children's homework and bedtime then and will be unable to come to the telephone.'

That's how Tessa and Francis 'do it', but I'm afraid that if I tried to pretend that's how I did it my friends would laugh at me.

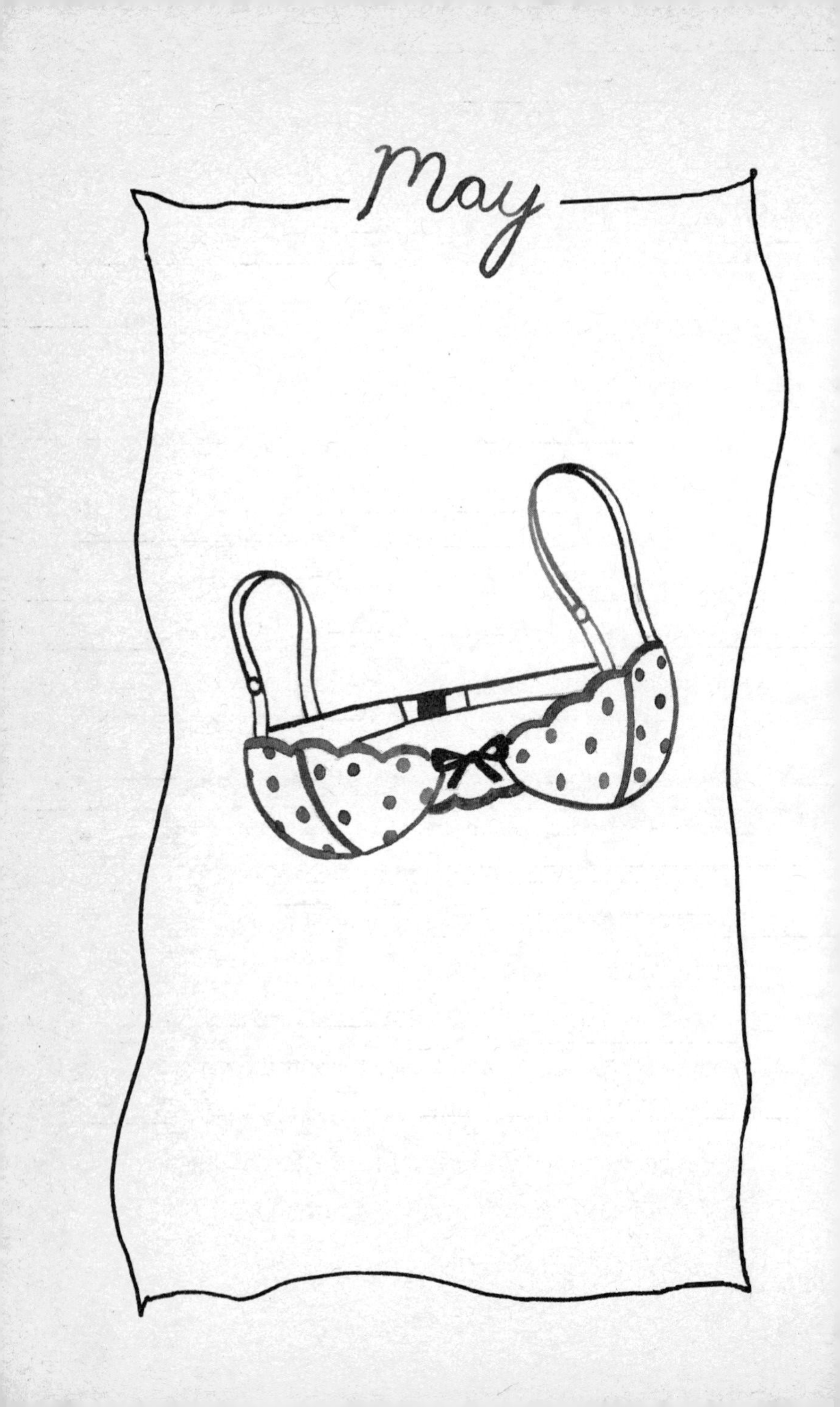
May

May

It's time to meet my friend Kate, I fear.

Kate has three children under eight, makes her own plum jam with her own fruit, is class rep for Year Two, and, before you say 'I don't know how she does it' (and I've told you in great detail how I 'do it' already), I should add that Kate is the most successful female venture capitalist in Europe. Aren't you loving her already?

I was at school and university with Kate (first and lacrosse blue) and we spent some of half-term with her in Wales.

I received an email called 'Welsh activities' from her the week before half-term. It went like this: 'Tuesday: 1000 kayaking into Hay-on-Wye (picnic lunch en route); 1300 Jacqueline Wilson event at Hay Festival; 1500 riding; 1800 mountain biking/boarding; 1930 boules and Pimms. Wednesday: 1000 take pony up mountain (picnic lunch at summit); 1400 riding . . .' etc.

I forwarded the email to my husband and after a pregnant interval he responded with enthusiasm.

'I'm not coming,' his email said.

But I was longing to go. I was keen to show Kate, who is bliss, what a tremendous mucker-inner I am, and how I am truly a country girl rather than a snotty-nosed townie at heart, what with my family farm in deepest Exmoor, etc. So we went.

When we arrived in convoy at Aberedw on Monday evening (my husband insists on bringing his Audi, so he has a getaway car at all times), Kate's children were gambolling by the river. Tommy the pony was even more picturesquely in the kitchen, where the long oak table sparkled with an encouraging array of wine glasses.

Our three children unfurled themselves and ran with exultant cries over a rope suspension bridge to a treehouse set high up in the hill, which had sleeping-bags laid out on the wooden floor and a

Poussin-like view down the valley. The schedule of Welsh activities then went: 2030 riding the zip-wire and Tommy; 2130 sit down to delicious dinner cooked by our hosts; 2400 bed.

In the morning, Kate was up with the lark and through my hangover I could hear the noisy clatter of six children eating cereal. I made my way to the kitchen where Kate was flipping pancakes on the hotplate of the Aga. She was in a crop-top and shorts and had already been for a run. 'Sleep well? How are you?' she cried, as the batter sizzled.

'It's a bit too early to tell,' I whispered, already feeling wimpy in comparison. By the time I had made coffee, Kate had got all the children dressed and sitting playing chess and writing stories at the kitchen table. She then disappeared, but when I looked out of the window I could see she had tacked up Tommy and was running alongside the pony, while my daughter trotted up and down, blonde locks flying.

When I emerged from my shower, Kate had got all the children into the van for the 1000 kayaking activity and had packed two bags, one with dry clothes, the other with a picnic. We headed to Glasbury. Kate repacked the kit into two watertight blue plastic drums and we transhipped into canoes and kayaks. I took her daughter and my sons and we paddled off to the festival in Hay-on-Wye for the 1300 literary activity. The river was quite high and, just before we stopped midway on a grassy bank for our picnic, my canoe went longways in a rapid and lodged against a submerged tree.

Sighing, I very carefully removed my sneakers and rolled up my trousers and stepped into the torrent to try to jiggle the canoe away from the tree. But I was too weak. I looked over for the others. Kate stood up, dived fully dressed into the Wye and freestyled towards me. Seconds later, she had freed my laden canoe.

By the time I had got the children on to the bank, Kate (who recently turned down an invitation to Chequers – too busy) had made a fire and was frying sausages. A kettle was boiling for tea. 'So, Kate,' I asked, in a leading way, 'what did you think of *I Don't Know How She Does It*?' (spotted on bookshelf in her millhouse in Aberedw).

Kate finished her sausage roll before replying. 'I liked the bit about her distressing the mince pies,' she said, 'but the rest got up my nose. The Kate Reddy person was doing a crap job in the City and the message seemed to be that, if it all got a bit much, the best option for women was to give it all up.'

Next day, on the train back to London, Kate (who was in loco parentis) got my son to do two solid hours of geography revision, and my admiration of her has risen to hot-making levels. Kate Reddy is deservedly famous all over the world, but I am even happier to bring you a real Superwoman, alive and well and weekending near Hay-on-Wye.

May

I was keen to press on with a round-up of school news (we are still deep in the process of looking at secondary schools for son one), but first, an update on the Kate situation.

I have had a rather mixed response from friends to my ecstatic accounts of Kate the Superwoman and our weekend in Wales.

'Just shut up about Kate, will you?' snapped my friend Jenni, who used to edit *Channel Four News* and is a bit of a super-achiever herself. 'You want to know how my schedule of weekend activities goes? It goes eat, sleep, read newspapers, eat, sleep, eat, sleep. I don't wanna *hear* about this woman!'

So then, of course, I had to torture Jenni further. Rather than shut up, I told her about the time when, during one of our two riding activities, I had a rather bad fall from my horse, Merlin, and was thrown on to my back into a patch of gorse and blacked out. When I opened my eyes, I saw stars, felt the thundering of hooves and then saw Kate galloping to my rescue like a Valkyrie.

In the middle of telling Jenni this, she started

making an alarming choking noise down the phone, so I had to stop in case I triggered some sort of nervous collapse.

Still, the Kate thing (men want to marry her and women want to kill her) has made me think about 'mommy wars' – that lovely American phrase for the vicious dispute between stay-at-home mothers 'doing kids' and those who work outside the home.

For some reason, we have accepted the propaganda peddled by the stay-at-home mothers (who like to call themselves 'home managers') that they are the busy bees. It is only the 'home managers', we are told, who host toddler music-and-movement groups, run the school fête, organize charity quizzes, and do all the other unpaid stuff that makes the world go round and a better place 'for all our children'.

I don't deny that there is some truth in this, but it's not the whole story. Look, if you can bear to again, at Kate. She is, as I mentioned, class rep for Year Two, but when our school reunion came round, who volunteered to organize it? Kate. And when the assisted-places scholarship fund was set up a few weeks ago, who volunteered to take on the fundraising drive and cocktail party? You got it. Kate.

Well, I just bumped into my daughter's lovely, efficient, mother-of-four class rep, Alison, at the swimming pool. Alison spotted me, moved in for the kill and asked me if I wanted to take over next year, explaining that she had done it for two whole years.

'What does it involve?' I said, playing for time, the familiar icy hand gripping my vitals. 'Oh, not much,' said Alison, hope in her voice. 'Traffic duty rota . . . Nit check . . . PTA meetings . . . Coffee mornings, updating databases . . . It's not too burdensome.'

I return to my theme. In my experience, the distinction between working mothers and 'home managers' is a false one.

Kate, a full-time working mother, made her son's birthday cake at midnight the other night. My daughter has a bake sale at school tomorrow and I (a stay-at-home mother, but not a full-time

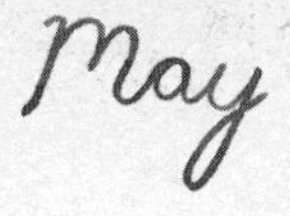

housewife) am outsourcing this chore to Lord Sainsbury. And Alison, sorry, but I must decline once again your invitation to be Year Five class rep, although I know I could always fit it in between dog-walking, the school run and all the other duties I manage to cram in, like the Prime Minister, in the course of my busy day.

No, I'm afraid the world pretty much divides into doers and slackers, into those who can and do and those who can but don't.

And I should know.

Please don't ask why, but my youngest son, Oliver, aged six, has suddenly joined his ten-year-old brother at school in Swiss Cottage, a nerve-shredding twenty-five-minute drive away. (Oh, all right then, if you must know, a place came up and we would miss it unless we moved fast.)

'At least you won't have three in three different schools any longer,' I am told. I don't have the energy to explain that, effectively, I still do.

For the junior school is separated by a quarter-mile of bumper-to-bumper traffic from the senior school. And Ludo's school day is from 8.10 a.m. to 3.50 p.m., and Oliver's is from 8.30 a.m. to 3.30 p.m. Now, it is true that I have a permit from Camden that allows me to park in a 300-yard radius of the school for fifteen minutes during drop-off and pick-up.

But the problem is, as you have no doubt worked out, that drop-off and pick-up alone takes half an hour – i.e., twice the length of my permitted fifteen-minute stay. So I have to park on a meter somewhere near Primrose Hill, and trudge, carrying a trumpet, schoolbags and sports kit, and harrying the boys, not to get a ticket. Handy, that.

The other gloriously convenient aspect is that, with both boys at effectively two different schools, no one wants to do a school run with me, although they are far too polite to say so.

May

But this was not yet clear at our school-run planning meeting, I now recall, which was rather disturbingly joined for the first time by a father, an Internet wunderkind, whom I shall call Josh. His son had just started in the 'middle' school, which is – though this does not need to detain us now – in a third location in Swiss Cottage.

There we were, the four of us, three women and Josh, trying to sort out the rota over biscuits and herbal tea. While we three women knew we were in for a long haul, followed by nightly conference calls, and weeks of snagging, the new father was going for a result.

You bet he was. He analysed the variables. He set out, in his words, the 'parameters of the problem'. He suggested 'ways forward' and mediated a short discussion of whether a morning run and an afternoon run held the same 'value', given traffic flows. He offered to create a spreadsheet. At one point, he significantly glanced at his watch and summarized what we could 'take away' from the meeting in a succinct two-point plan. Like many men, he thought that if you applied yourself scientifically to a problem you would find a solution.

But, as far as I could see, there wasn't one. There were five children to ferry, and two of the mothers could only (would only – I kept saying things like, 'When I was a child we just rattled around the back and no one bothered with seatbelts,' to hollow laughs and raised eyebrows) take four in their runabouts; there were after-school clubs to factor in; and then there was the junior-school nightmare, the unwelcome extra I was bringing to the party this year.

'Look,' I intervened, an hour into the session, because I could see our feminine inability to apply Vulcan logic and a Kantian perspective to the school run was becoming irksome to Josh.

'I can see it's a real bore, this fiddling around at the junior school. I'm really sorry. So I propose that I do one more run a week than you three to compensate.' I congratulated myself on my generosity (which I was satisfied would not be accepted) and problem-solving capability, and helped myself to a biscuit.

'But you should be doing twice as many runs as us anyway,' replied another mother. 'You have two boys and we all only have one child at the school each. That's how they do it at Bute House.' (Bute House is the super-posh prep school that my daughter unaccountably failed to get into but all my friends' daughters did, thanks to me).

The penny dropped. This was constructive dismissal. If I was going to have to do twice as many runs as everyone else, on any cost-benefit analysis, I might as well do it on my own. Of course!

I was the structural impediment, and once I was gone the school run could run smoothly. The annoying thing was, I realized as I watched Josh sip his tea in triumph, that he had clearly worked out this solution (perfect for them, dreadful for me) hours before.

So my husband and I are managing, up to a point. But this week, he called me from the car. 'I had to hang around for ages at the junior school,' he complained. 'And I had to leave the car on a double yellow, too. I almost got a ticket! This is bloody hopeless, isn't it?'

I could have replied, 'Yes, it is hopeless, and stressful, and time-consuming. Well spotted. And?' etc. But I am holding fire. I think it's quite possible that, as a male, he will be so enraged by the structural inefficiencies of the system, which requires us to drive two boys to the same school at two different locations and at two different times twice a day, that he will sort it out.

But I also think it's quite possible that not even my husband will share my school run with me.

There are various bits of paper floating about my desk, to add to the general sense of panic and chaos.

There's the letter from our nice lady vicar, which

was enclosed with the new Sunday School rota, thanking me for my 'contribution towards our Sunday worship'. It went on to mention, *en passant*, that she was sure I had noticed what a 'big difference' it made when stewarding, readings, Sunday School and so forth went smoothly and 'how disruptive' it could be if people dropped out.

I feel, guiltily, that this letter is aimed at me. I went down to Wales and Exmoor for half-term and missed my Sunday School teaching slot. This meant that someone else had to try, impromptu, to explain the Virgin Birth to twenty rowdy under-eights with only some dead Pritt Sticks and a bucket of topless felt-pens for company.

I took my punishment, though, the following week, when I leapt into the breach and covered for someone else. The sermon was the Holy Trinity, a subject of ineffable mystery that the finest theological minds in the land have failed to explain satisfactorily, and so, now, have I. After the children had cut out their clover leaves (inspired, eh?) from green card in three minutes flat, the rest of the service went by pretty slowly, I can tell you.

Now, in principle I have nothing against being an active parishioner, and am as ready as the next parent to participate in what we now call the 'school community'. Fair's fair, we've all got to do our share, and if you want something done ask a busy woman, and so on. But as far as I can see, if you don't draw the line somewhere (as I had to last week over the sweet offer Alison made to me to be class rep for the next two years) it can take over your life.

'I now understand the sheer hell that is being a W11 mummy,' my husband announced as he came downstairs to make a pot of Lapsang after his afternoon nap one day last week. (He was having a day at home and had therefore spent the morning teasing me about my busy day at the gym and meeting a girlfriend for coffee.) 'All I need now is a big, strong banker to take care of me and life would be complete.'

May

We have been school-hunting for my ten-year-old son, who wants (sob) to board at thirteen. So we have blanked our minds to the sick-making sums of money involved and toured the country. I've seen seven schools, and my husband nine (he has done Sherborne and Oundle, solo). I can also add Bryanston to my score, because I was there for a spell before being invited to leave (my housemaster would send my parents polite letters wondering whether they had yet 'had any success in finding another school' for me). When it comes to my baby going to boarding school, believe me, I'm not letting my fingers just do the walking through *The Good Schools Guide*. We go together, man and wife, showing a united front, and roll up for the grand tour, which climaxes with a session with the headmaster, who is invariably leaving the year before our son will get there. It's a fine way, I can tell you, of spending the hours I have spare between chauffeuring the boys from Notting Hill to their prep school in Hampstead, so let me pass on some tips.

It's not a good idea to bring Junior to his prospective school. After two hours trailing around the science block and fives courts, your child is going to be a husk of his usual charming, chatty self. At Charterhouse, our darling son sat slumped almost comatose in his armchair after an arduous tour that included a good twenty minutes at the climbing wall.

I darted him dagger looks to try to get him to sit up and look lively, but I don't think any of us (and, don't forget, they are interviewing parents as much as pupils) came across as prime Carthusian material.

Be brazen enough to ask for the greatest hits. If a request to skip the new indoor Olympic swimming pool and interactive design-technology centre is met with a raised eyebrow, you have your answer ready.

'Of course, it's not that we don't want to see the multi-sports centre, good Lord, no,' you cry. 'It's just that we know that education is all about [pause as you look deep into your son's possible future housemaster's eyes] the teaching, not the facilities. It's the people, isn't it?'

Sometimes it's impossible to decline to take a two-mile detour to see the pottery workshop or golf course (they are mad keen for you to see the sumptuous facilities as you are shelling out twenty thou a year), but do try to see the dining-hall, the chapel, a boarding-house and as many of the teaching staff and pupils as possible.

Then comes the hard part: working out which one is right for your child. In my experience, school shopping is about as straightforward as buying bras.

Last week, taking a break from school visits, I dropped into Rigby & Peller, corsetière to the Queen. I was ushered into a carpeted, curtained cubicle by a small Portuguese woman, who asked me what I wanted and in what size.

'Bras,' I replied, confidently, '36B.' She asked me to disrobe to the waist. She whipped a tape measure around my ribcage, weighed me up with a raking glance and disappeared, returning with a selection of undergarments.

She held one up in front of me, so I put my arms through the armholes, thereby pitching myself forwards. As I did so, she expertly eased my embonpoint into the cups, nipped behind me to rearrange things manually – paying particular attention to the lie of the seams – and then did up the back. We then both gazed at my prouder reflection in the mirror.

'So, what size is this?' I asked, as she unhooked one bra and we went through the routine for the next one. 'Crumbs!' was all I could manage when she told me. 'Am I really?'

So there we go. You go through life thinking one thing and it turns out you were wrong all along. One size does not fit all. The customer is not always right. And when it comes to choosing your child's school, my last tip is to allow yourself to be guided towards the best fit by the true professionals, be it your son's head teacher or the nice woman at Rigby & Peller, because it will be a real weight off your chest.

I will leave you with that uplifting thought.

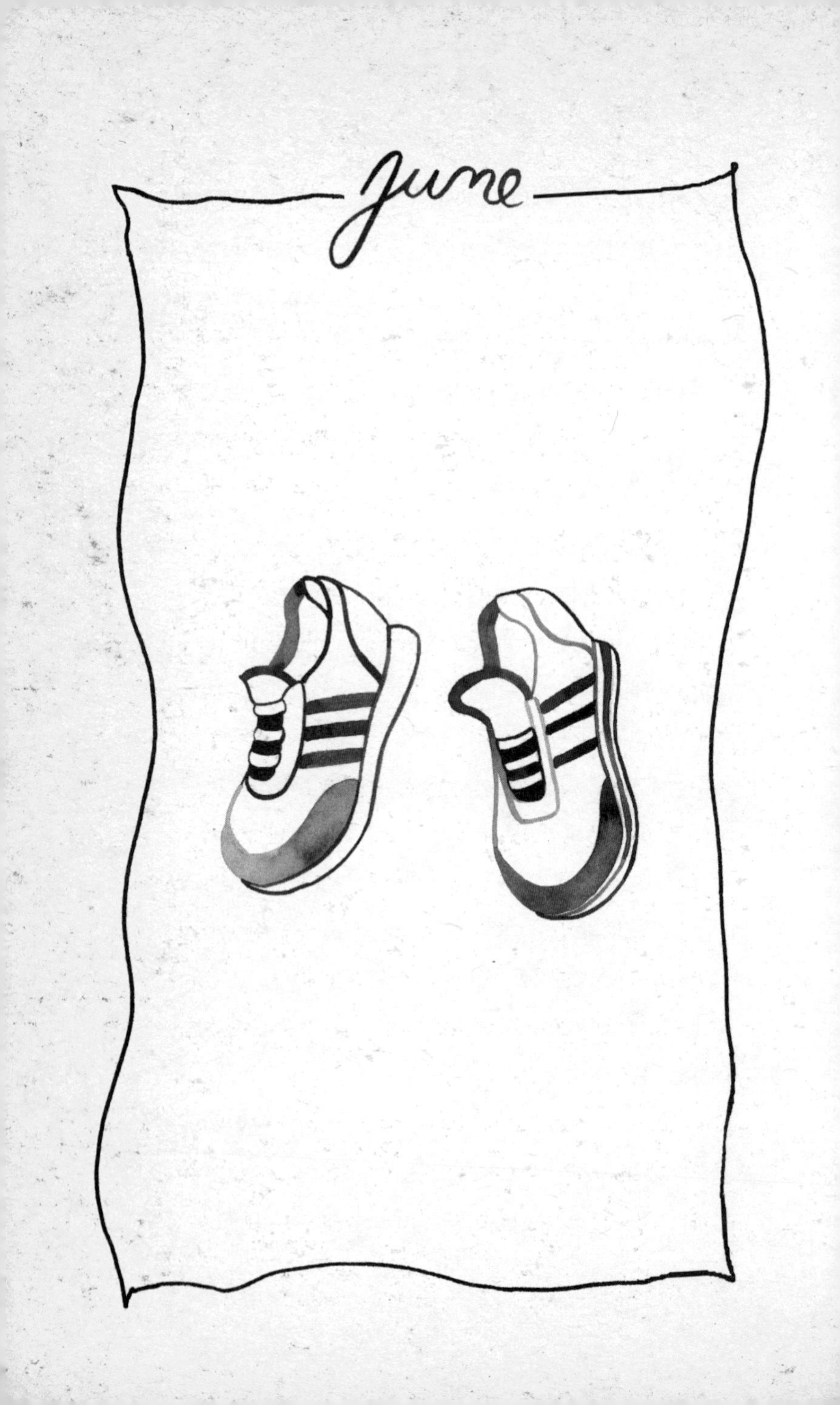
June

June

One sports day down, three to go.

On Tuesday, it was my son's sports day, held on the sports track on Hampstead Heath, an event that last year left my husband nursing a mysterious male complaint he called 'double groin strain' and unable to climb stairs for a fortnight. I did very badly in the mothers' race, a fact that I put down to the professionalism of North London mummies, who are not, on the whole, the picnic-hamper-and-floral-frock type, but tend to pitch up in sports bras and running shorts, with little backpacks containing high-energy drinks and glucose 'power' bars (and that's just for them).

I regard them as having a very unfair advantage over us stay-at-home mothers/home managers, because they have all been limbering up like crazy by getting up at 6.30 a.m., doing the school run, running or biking to their offices, showering and changing into their separates from Episode, and then taking the Tube home again in ninety-five-degree heat to supervise homework. I mean, how unfair is that?

Today, it's our annual communal-garden sports and fun-filled family day, to which we all look forward with keen anticipation. It starts with the sports at about 2 p.m. and ends with vigorous disco-dancing for grown-ups at about midnight in a marquee erected at the far end of the greensward from us.

I am in the habit of very graciously asking friends to dinner on this midsummer's night, on the grounds that it must be such a treat for them to come to our heavenly communal garden to mingle with my charming neighbours. As I invite them, I remind them that this garden party is my one stab at 'social inclusion' of the season, ha ha!

'Not that ghastly garden thing again,' groaned one dear friend, when I invited him and his wife for the second year running, 'when you all wander around sniffing the honeysuckle and congratulating each other for living on a communal garden in Notting Hill.'

'But it's really good fun. My neighbours are really nice,' I went on, because the friend, after describing tonight's festivities as 'an orgy of smugness', eventually declined, pleading a pressing subsequent engagement.

I don't usually invite friends to the afternoon sports beforehand, for reasons that will become clear.

For children, there's the egg-and-spoon, running races, sack races and the three-legged race. For adults, there's a sprinting race for the sixteen- to thirty-nine-year-olds and one for the over-forties, with male and female heats for both. The marathon – when everyone runs around the perimeter of the garden – was sadly abandoned a few years ago when one highly competitive banker was seen cutting a corner and then tripping up another highly competitive banker, who ended up in hospital having gravel picked out of his knees.

I am, I fear, known to have 'form' when it comes to these athletic little contests between close neighbours. How can I forget that two years ago one friend on the garden called me a 'bitch' when I won the sixteen to thirty-nine race and another neighbour went about the party later saying I bolted at 'Steady' instead of 'Go!', which was a hurtful slander.

Last year, I won the race again. My husband puts my triumph down to my 'aerodynamic nose'. I don't know about that, but it was most unfortunate for the poor woman ahead of me that I touched her leg totally by accident and she stumbled just before the finishing line.

Anyway, if all the leggy teens on the garden consider it way too sad to compete, I might just win for the third year running, because most of my main opponents have, I note, just moved up into the over-forty age bracket, leaving the under-forty field to me.

My winning technique is this. When the race is called, I shyly hang back, as my children shout: 'Come on, Mummy! Please!' I make modest protests. As the clamour from my family mounts, I cave in with a look that says 'At least I'm a good sport' and line up for the race, arranging my children on the finishing line opposite me. Then I groan loudly to the other mothers about how embarrassing this is, how unfit I am and that I haven't been to the gym all year. This bit is very important.

Then, at the off, something strange happens. I feel the force of my children's will for me to win and run. Elbows out, tripping up anyone who comes near, I breast the tape into the arms of my cheering children.

It's so comforting to see that, for them, too, the winning takes second place to the taking part.

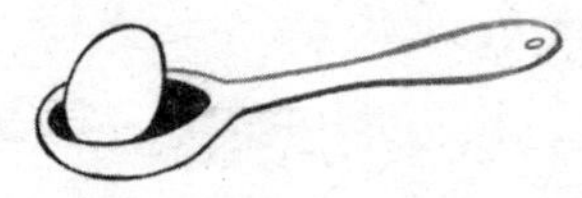

I was in the kitchen putting carrot batons from Planet Organic into little wooden bowls for snacks when Ludo came running in from the communal garden, bawling, one sultry afternoon last week.

'Darling,' I cried out. 'What's happened?' After giving me a brief, narrow look, my son explained that he had got into a fight with another boy, Nat, an invited guest of another child who lived along the crescent.

'He used the f-word and started kicking me,' my son sobbed. 'So I pushed him over and told him to jolly well pick on someone his own size.'

I switched into Miss Marple mode – i.e., from maternal to forensic.

'How old is Nat?' I asked, imagining I might have to tackle some sneering teen in Quiksilver shorts with body piercings.

'I dunno,' sobbed my eldest son, ever more loudly. 'And then the mummy came out and ticked me off and told me to apologize and she was ever so mean to me.' (He was watching my face through his tears to monitor my reaction to all this.)

You know when you think someone has done something unjust to your child? In my case, not only does the red mist descend, but I also become seriously swivel-eyed.

'Right,' I said, slamming the fridge shut. 'I'm going to sort this out.'

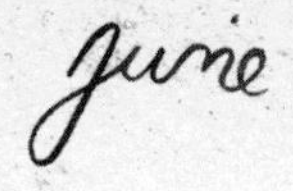

We marched as to war into the communal garden. I carried the carrot batons as a sort of shield in front of me.

Through the hazy heat, I could dimly make out a small group at the far end.

There was the neighbour's son, Adam, and a boy I took to be Nat, and a woman wearing an itsy-bitsy thong-style bikini.

The child was not, I saw instantly with dismay, some hulking brute. He was tiny, and not only was he tiny but he had corkscrew black curls and skin the colour of a Starbucks frappuccino, too. And he was all of six years old.

This was bad. Though I viscerally believed every word my son had told me, the truth remained.

Even if Nat was the devil-child from hell, my son was much older than him, and therefore, in the eyes of the other mummy, and right-thinking society, a horrid, big, bad rabbit.

'Um,' I began nonetheless, 'has there been some sort of altercation?'

As the word slipped from my lips, I was cursing

myself. Why couldn't I just say 'problem'? The woman stared me down. She had honey-blonde hair and her bronzed skin glistened with oil and droplets of water. As well it might, as she was playing suggestively with a garden hose. The two boys stood by, hoping she might fill their paddling pool.

'Yes, there most certainly has,' she retorted. 'My son came in crying and saying your son had pushed him over on to the pebbly path. As the only adult present I explained that, if he wanted to play with Nat again, he should first apologize.' She twitched the hose, spraying my new suede flip-flops, before delivering what I assumed was the *coup de grâce*. 'I always expect other parents to discipline my own child if they've done something wrong, don't you?'

I was just wondering exactly how I was going to kill her when Oliver rushed up, howling, with one of his tiny 'owies'. As I examined his minute graze, distracted, I heard her snap: 'Hello? Am I talking to myself here?'

And oh, how I wish I had lashed back and said that,

when I took it on myself to 'discipline' other people's children, I managed not to reduce them to tears.

And that, since neither of us had been in the garden at the time, it had been most presumptuous of her to assume that my son had been the aggressor, even if he was older. And, while we were at it, why on earth was she cavorting about in a bikini and flaunting her buffness in front of other people's husbands?

Right on cue, my husband came towards us, but I headed him off. I sat him down and briefed him on the pebbly-path incident. When I got to the bit about her saying snippily 'Am I talking to myself here?' he chuckled in recognition (he also frequently claims to address me and receive no response).

Nat and Adam were soon called in to tea. As they trotted off we heard a familiar voice.

'Boys! I want the paddling pool and the waterguns and the swingball, now, before tea!'

I clutched at my husband in gleeful anticipation.

'Heh heh,' I sniggered. 'As if! Bet they don't come out for the stuff. Ha ha!' And I waited for the bikini woman to suffer the ritual humiliation of being disobeyed, in public, by one's own children.

But Nat raced out. He gathered an armful of stuff and disappeared into the house. Then came that authoritative voice, raised again.

'And the swingball, I said.' So then I was forced to watch as Nat struggled past yet again with the swingball.

And her triumph, I suppose, was complete when my husband remarked (as Nat trotted out for the last Supersoaker): 'I do love to see a parent exercising a little authority for once, don't you?'

Oliver has lost his trainers in the communal garden.

I realize that this announcement has all the shock value of a news story headlined 'Baby's bonnet found on railing', so let me rephrase that. Oliver has lost his trainers, the ones that contained his orthotics – little shaped inserts that had been moulded from a cast of his own foot. Don't ask me why he has orthotics; I'm not a podiatrist. I can, though, tell you exactly how much they cost, because I lie in bed at night wondering where on earth his £27 Start-Rites, housing the £447 orthotics, could be.

I have searched high and low, particularly in the garden, a treasure-trove of socks, old tennis balls and unmarked items of school uniform. I pick up any of my own children's effects and arrange single socks on a bench. But, so far, there have been no sightings of Oliver's trainers. Which is odd, because he was wearing them when he came home from school and the only place he's been, to my knowledge, is in the garden.

I say 'to my knowledge' because when he goes into the garden he melts away, particularly at mealtimes, when he suspects that I may not be serving the only solid food he will eat (Cheerios and pasta pesto). A protracted search, requiring much name-calling and telephone calls, usually locates him in a neighbouring house. Oliver's a kibbutznik. He thinks that everyone else's houses are an extension of his and that everyone else's parents will indulge him as much as I do.

Once, one of our neighbours, a solicitor aged sixty, gave Oliver, who is six, a piece of chewing gum when we bumped into him on our way to school.

Oliver does not like chewing gum, but he was clearly impressed by the gesture, for many months later Oliver left our house, crossed the garden and entered the solicitor's house by the back door.

There was no one in the downstairs kitchen, so he turned on the television and sat there happily watching *The Fimbles*. After a while, he wandered upstairs. There was no one on the ground floor, nor on the first floor. Eventually, he came across a study in the attic, where Michael was working at a desk facing the window.

'Can I have some more chewing gum?' he asked, standing in the doorway. Michael swivelled around. He had been on the telephone and had not heard Oliver's ascent. 'Oh, hello, Oliver,' said Michael, only slightly surprised, he told me later, to find one of the many children who lived on the garden standing in his study at that hour. 'Actually, I don't have any at the moment.' Oliver was undeterred by this answer, even though it was not the one he was looking for.

'Well canive some sweets then?' he persisted.

'I'm afraid I don't have any sweets either,' said Michael. 'I'm awfully sorry.'

'Well just give me some money, then,' Oliver said, his patience finally cracking, 'so I can go and buy some!'

It was a long shot, but I asked Michael if he has Oliver's trainers. He doesn't and nor do the other obvious candidates (the neighbours with the PlayStation and those with satellite television). So I have bought new ones.

But the loss of the orthotics is hard to bear. As we paid for them with real money (my health insurer wouldn't pay, on the grounds that any ailment my family suffers is automatically excluded from our £300-a-month health policy), their disappearance has filled me with panic. I have not begun the long, expensive process of getting new ones cast because, if

I do, the old ones will doubtless turn up, just as infertile couples fall pregnant with twins as soon as they finally get the green light to adopt.

But I must face the worst. My late grandmother used to wear hearing aids that looked like rubbery pink snails, but she was more often without them because, if she ever left one lying around, the terriers would eat it. I was reminded of this when I found my daughter's new shoes in the garden yesterday morning. They had been left there overnight and foxes had gnawed off the straps, and so I have just made yet another shopping trip to replace them.

So *j'accuse* the foxes. Foxes love chewing leather straps, and as for bitesize, felty orthotics perfumed by the soles of Oliver's tender young feet . . . mmm! I was quite tempted to give them a nibble myself.

June

One of the hazards of living in Notting Hill (apart from catfights between alpha mummies in the communal garden) is the presence in the 'hood' of so many real live celebrities. Even though I have lived here on and off since 1979, I haven't yet learnt the New York trick of giving a celeb plenty of space. I can go regrettably ga-ga when a celebrity is in radius.

I still break out in a sweat when I remember the time Milly was invited to Ruby Wax's daughter's birthday party.

As you can imagine, this was a red-letter day for me. I cleared my schedule and meanly stood down my then nanny so that it would be me taking Milly to the princess party, not her. At the appointed hour we entered a star-spangled, wand-waving scrum of small girls in pink net dresses with fairy wings. Apart from Ruby and Ruby's nanny, I recognized no one.

Any sensible, non-starstruck person would have shoved Milly briskly into the throng and legged it. But as I had (I cringe to report) actually taken time off work to be there, I felt I had invested in this occasion.

June

'So which one is yours?' I asked a woman who was lifting the clingfilm from a plate of sandwiches and sneaking one towards her mouth. 'I'm the nanny,' she said. 'Oh! How nice,' I replied, my eyes swivelling about to see who I was going to collar next. 'I'm Milly's mum.' 'I know you are,' the nanny replied shortly. 'I see you at circle time, every day.'

And so it went. I had a miserable time because I was the only mother there apart from Ruby, who didn't exactly make a beeline for me, and the nannies had a miserable time with me there because, as I was present, they could not compare pay and conditions.

If it's hard being the only mummy at a nannies-only party, it's even harder being an unkempt, civilian mummy in celebrityville. Especially when I'm with the children, because then I make the fatal mistake of putting myself in their shoes. 'Darling!' I hissed to Ludo in Tesco the other day. 'That's Will Young!' And so it was. 'Don't you want to say hello?' I whispered. 'No . . . OK,' he said, scuffing a shoe.

So I introduced Ludo. But Will had a hunted,

desperate look in his eyes. 'I'm a bit ill at the moment. Sorry,' he whispered, and darted away.

This half-term started with a horrid visit to the dentist (and, if the eyes are the windows to the soul, your children's teeth are the monument to your mothering skills). Afterwards, we repaired to Starbucks in Holland Park. As I was consoling the still-crabby children for their fillings with hot chocolate and muffins, my celebrity radar suddenly pinged. Wasn't that thin young man with deep lines around his mouth Robbie Williams? I went back to our sofa and said, 'Don't stare, OK, but that guy in the cap is Robbie Williams.'

The children carried on spooning the whipped cream from their hot chocolate imperturbably. They are so blasé they did not even look up, apart from to check that it was indeed Robbie and I wasn't teasing. But as I was fetching my coffee from the counter, where Robbie and pal were waiting, Oliver surged up. 'Who did you say it was, Mummy?' he shouted.

'It's Robbie Williams, darling,' I hissed.

Robbie stared levelly at me, in fury. Then he looked down at Oliver. I gabbled, assuming that Robbie would find Oliver irresistible: 'He lives in the next street and you rang his doorbell when we went trick or treating.'

Aaaaargh! I had done it again! I had wrongly assumed that someone famous wanted to be reminded of the fact. Robbie said nothing, which was just as well, because I had made it all up and all of us, including Oliver, knew that I was raving. 'No, I didn't ring your bloody bell,' he said, giving Robbie Williams a look, and stormed back to the sofa.

I've raised my children to be so democratic, in a Notting-Hilly sort of way, don't you think? They're just as rude to celebrities as they are to anyone else.

June

We were crawling through Hyde Park during last weekend's heatwave, on our way to the Serpentine.

'I'm hungry. Are we nearly there?' came the welcome cry.

'For goodness' sake,' I hissed. 'You'd think we were driving to Wales. We've only been in the car fifteen minutes. But, as it's two o'clock, we'll have our picnic in the car.'

I reached down and started passing the sandwiches back to the children, making sure I reserved the expensive deluxe one with rocket and crayfish for myself (the children prefer petrol-station sandwiches to those from Prét à Manger). We all started munching. Peace was restored. A call came through on my mobile. As we were motionless in traffic, I took it, and enjoyed a long gossip with a girlfriend while inching forward in the baking heat, one arm dangling in the sunshine.

Just as we were going over the bridge, a police car overtook us. As I had my belt on and had stowed my mobile, I thought nothing of it. But the car then slewed in front of us, blocking our way and the crawl of traffic.

A policeman came over, and glowered down. I gazed up at him innocently, wondering whether he was going to tell me something about a brake light, and thought what a heart-warming sight we must present: three tow-headed, smiling and well-fed children, on their way to enjoy the healthful amenity of a Royal Park on a sunny day, in a taxed, roadworthy vehicle driven by a law-abiding, responsible adult.

'I've a good mind to book you, madam, for dangerous driving,' he said, to my shock, in an unpleasant voice. 'What on earth do you think you were doing back there?'

And then I made my mistake. I didn't follow the infallible rule of intercourse with law-enforcers, as perfected by Paris Hilton (she is so sweetly apologetic that she ends up being asked out to dinner by the highway cops instead of being booked for speeding at 150 kph on the freeway while affixing her false-eyelashes).

'I beg your pardon! The traffic's barely moving!' I

couldn't help whining, instead. 'How could I be driving dangerously at five miles an hour when the traffic's virtually at a standstill?'

That, of course, was asking for it. The policeman whipped out a notebook in order to inform me I had committed the following offences: 1) Failing to stay within my lane. 2) Taking one hand off the wheel while holding a mobile telephone. 3) Speaking into a hand-held mobile while driving.

But there was more to come. In order to deliver his knockout blow, he carefully placed his notebook in his back pocket, removed his sunglasses, and puffed out his chest like a turkey-cock.

'And then, madam, you drove for some time with neither hand on the steering wheel at all,' he said, shaking his head.

I have to confess that at this point I marvelled at my own Douglas Bader-like ability to remain in control of a machine without the use of two vital limbs, but some mysterious intuition told me to keep my natural feelings of self-congratulation to myself.

'Did I?' I asked.

'Yes you did,' the officer snapped back. 'While you were opening your sandwiches. We've been following you since Bayswater.'

Well, he had me there. As anyone knows, it takes two hands, a set of teeth, and a razor-sharp panga to open a sandwich entombed in plastic, which is also handily child-proof. So I had opened them all on my lap, before handing them round. I must have been steering the car with my knees. Or perhaps my elbows – I couldn't remember.

All I do know is that I was in perfect control of my vehicle, just as RAF hero Sir Douglas Robert Steuart Bader was master of his Hawker Hurricane, even though he had two tin legs.

So I bit my lip, looked chastened, and said I was very, very sorry. I said it was all my fault, and I would not do it again. Sir.

So he grudgingly let me carry on.

As he proceeded in an orderly fashion back to his vehicle, to continue keeping the peace, I couldn't help noticing that he wasn't walking and chewing gum at the same time.

June

Some men just can't bear to see a woman multi-tasking, can they?

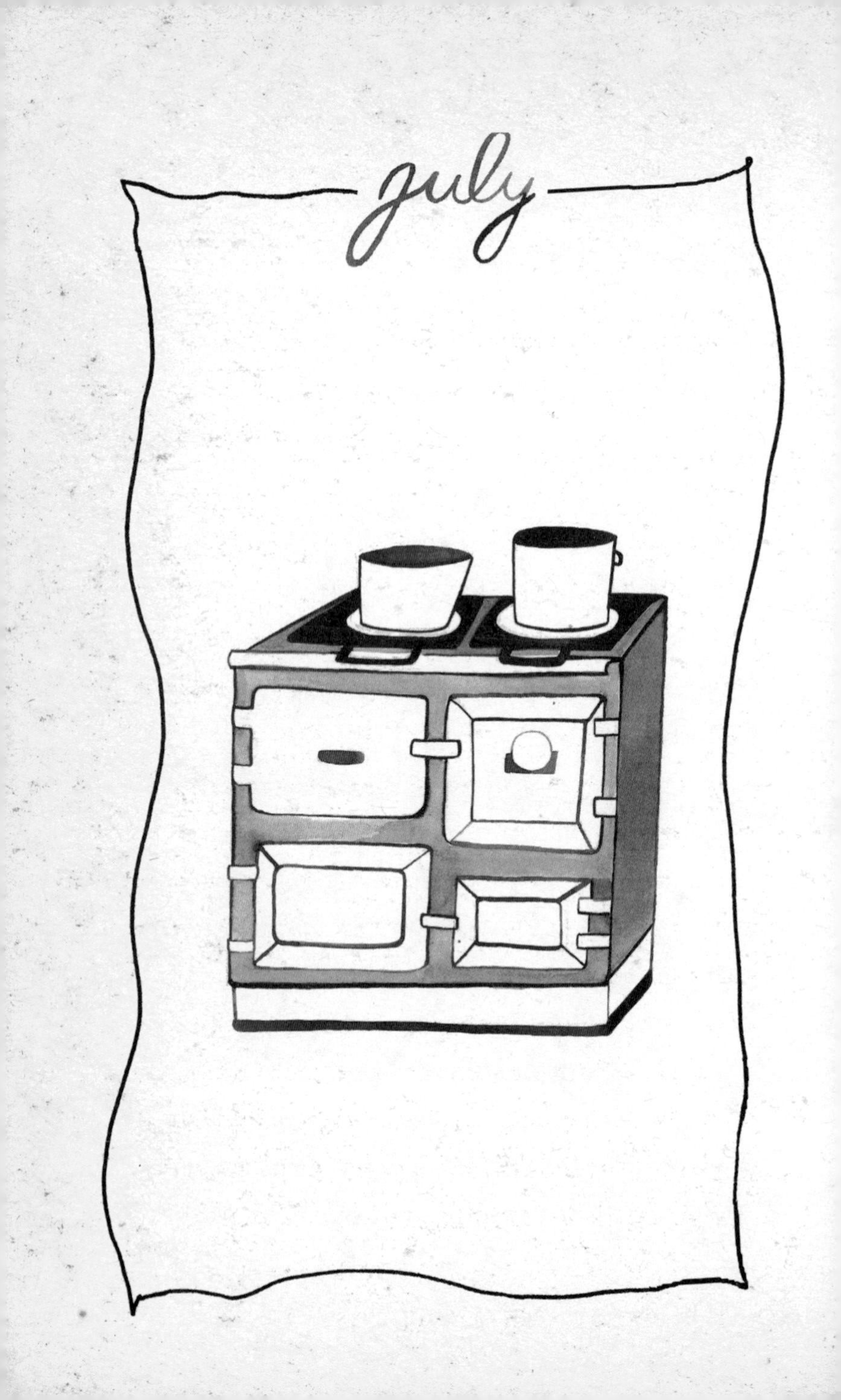
july

July

It is 9.30 a.m. I am hunched over my laptop in the darkened parlour of our farmhouse in deepest Somerset. I have to finish this diary entry in real time and within the hour, because the children will be back from the village at around 10.30 a.m.

My father, who lives up the lane, poked his head round our door after breakfast, made his signature cow-in-labour noise and offered to take a load of grandchildren to the whiz-bang Post Office-cum-store-cum-bank-cum-labour exchange that the plain old village shop used to be, to give me some time to write.

It takes twenty-five minutes to get to the village down our farm track. It takes ten minutes to buy three children the confectionery of their choice.

Which gives me exactly an hour, so I know that

those of you who are entertaining children, while also trying to work for the next eight weeks, will bear with me.

Shortly after the village posse returns, we have our next influx of guests from London. As Oli, our current guest, is still asleep upstairs in the spare bed, I cannot think about turning out the room.

It's at about this point in the summer that I can lose the will to live.

It's not that I don't love spending time with my children and guests. I do, and friends with children my children's age are nailed down up to a year in advance.

I send anxious, needy little emails and cards *pour mémoire* saying things like 'So looking forward to seeing you from 5 August to 9 August' with maps either enc. or attached.

It is 9.54 a.m. Just giving myself a time check. To recap: I've worked out how to get guests to arrive, and to leave. But what I still haven't worked out is the right answer to the 'What do you want me to bring?' question.

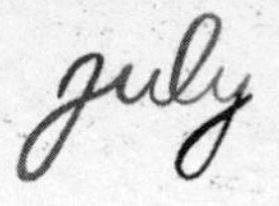

Bel, a TV producer, and Andrew, a barrister, plus their two nippers, were our first arrivals this summer.

'Do you want the honest answer?' I replied, when Bel asked. 'I want you to bring a case of wine, a huge hunk of Parmesan, and, really, as we don't have a tumble dryer, it would be fantastic if you could bring your own sheets and towels.'

'Fine!' cried Bel excitedly. 'And let me do a meal! Why don't I bring all the stuff for my mushroom risotto?'

I thought I heard a cow prolapsing again, but it turned out to be the sound of Andrew groaning out loud at the mention of Bel's risotto, much as my husband does when I threaten to make 'my couscous'.

But we were looking forward to their arrival very much. I thought we would even have the risotto the first night. As it was her special dish.

I had sent the directions by email to both of them (we live up a boneshaking two-mile track), but, even so, as they drew up in the yard after a four-hour drive from Camden Town, Andrew had the gritted smile of a man the undercarriage of whose new Alfa Romeo will never be honeymoon-fresh again.

After the cup of tea and tour of the west wing, we retired to the kitchen, where Andrew unloaded a large box of goodies. There was some lovely wine, and Bel had brought some duvets, but my beady eye could instantly see that the ingredients for the famous risotto she had mentioned had failed to materialize.

Now, the problem with our idyllic location is this: I cannot ask guests to pop out to the shops.

When Bel announced that she had forgotten the risotto stuff, I merely made a great song and dance about how we were all sooo much looking forward to it, and said there was nothing much else to eat apart from the tortellini I was planning to give to the children tomorrow.

'But that'll be all right for our supper!' I cried. 'Did you bring the Parmesan?' Bel's hand flew to her mouth.

'No problem,' said Andrew manfully, clearly trying

not to think of his dangling exhaust/sump. 'I'll go out for it. Where's the nearest Waitrose?'

'The nearest Waitrose!' I shrieked, hardly able to contain my delight. 'It's on the King's Road, I think.'

It's 10.30 a.m. Mooooo!

My father has returned with the children. Time's up.

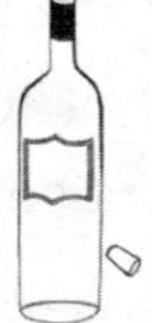

I have been sent a book by Bloomsbury, clearly in breathless anticipation of the looming summer break (the seven weeks, most of which I will spend here on Exmoor, will doubtless zip by in a flash!).

It is packed with wizard wheezes and feats of imagination, will be savoured by children and grown-ups alike, and it is, as you have no doubt guessed, an invaluable tool of a book: *I'm Bored!* by sisters Suzy Barratt and Polly Beard.

I came over all faint, though, when I saw that its

subtitle was *Over 100 inspiring and imaginative ideas for hours of fun with your children*, in much the same way I do whenever I see an Annabel Karmel cookbook. Mrs Karmel is the poster-mother for child nutrition who has made an enviable pile telling us to decorate homemade pizzas and biscuits with ‘smiley faces’ and make pasta sauces with ‘hidden’ vegetables. I don’t know about you, but this calls forth a horribly twee image of baby carrots playing hide and seek, calling out ‘Hiding!’ as they peek from the sauce.

As it happens, Hide and Seek, or ‘Hide and Go Peep’, as moms say in America, is one of the ‘original and entertaining’ ideas listed in *I’m Bored!*, along with I-Spy, Kim’s Game, Pooh Sticks, Doctors and Nurses, and Grandmother’s Footsteps.

My first original and entertaining observation about *I’m Bored!* is, therefore, that very little has come along in the keeping-children-happy stakes apart from dreaded GameBoys and computer games, DVDs, cable television and mall shopping. The games have not changed and the authors have managed to come up with only a few I hadn't played myself. I very much look forward to introducing Tree-Hugging and Celebrity-Spotting to my own grandchildren, Suzy and Polly!

My second observation is that this book is of the moment, in more ways than one. The activities can all be described in 100 words or so and the guiding principle seems to be that children (and, indeed, their mothers) get bored quickly.

The preparation for any activity is pared to a minimum, as is the projected time spent on it before your child will demand fresh entertainment. If preparation is needed, the authors are very apologetic. They point out that, in order for newspaper cut-outs to work, someone needs to cut out words from the newspaper first. Most games need no materials at all, presumably on the assumption that a child's attention span is not nearly long enough to encompass mummy finding the scissors and paper and actually making the paper dollies.

When I was a child (cue violins, etc.), my mother's equivalent of *I'm Bored!* was *Something to Do*, a pink Puffin paperback, illustrated by Shirley Hughes with delightful pen-and-ink drawings, and written by a collective of seven parents. Each month had a separate chapter, so the January chapter opens with a little poem called 'Winter Streams'. It continued with some folkloric information (Janus, first-footing, Twelfth Night) and had a special bird (the blue tit) and flower (snowdrop) to look out for each month.

As for activities – magical (violins swell to crescendo). Instead of celebrity-spotting (not a game, more an occupational hazard), we have 'making railway scenery'. There are immensely detailed instructions, which explain over three dense pages how to make hedges, telegraph poles and so on out of balsa and sponges. It ends: 'Now imagine you are 6 inches high and step into your newly made world.'

There is a long section on things you can make out of matchboxes, masses on doll's-house decorating, the rudiments of cooking and camping, bird-spotting and flower-pressing, and all manner of charming indoor, outdoor and beach pursuits, as well as a chapter (February) on things to do when you are ill in bed.

It is odd to think that once there was time for all this. My mother loved nothing more than spending a morning helping me make a pretty padded cover for a wire coat-hanger, say, while my elder brother played with his navy of boats made out of carved corks and my two younger brothers hit each other with cricket bats. But then, we had no television, lived in the country and my mother bought all my clothes for me until I was fifteen. Now, of course, my daughter, aged nine, chooses all her clothes and plays *Enter the Matrix* on a computer in her bedroom.

O tempora, o mores! The summer holidays may be interminable, but childhood is so much shorter (elegiac pause for reflection) than it used to be.

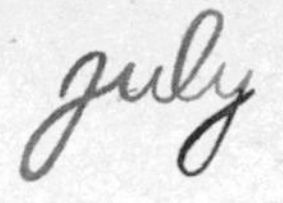

We have a New Yorker staying with us now, with her children. She arrived with boxes of blueberries and raspberries and asparagus and cheese, like the perfect house guest she is.

You'd hardly know she's not from these parts. She likes going for walks in the driving rain, stands gripping the Aga rail and warming her derrière against the roasting oven, and has even grasped my husband's complicated edicts about shutting all outside doors, but not the sitting-room door (if shut, it causes the house to fill with woodsmoke). And she likes slices of thickly buttered malt loaf washed down with many cups of tea.

One thing that makes Antonia different, though, is the fact that she is dating a film producer who lives in Los Angeles. The city is nine hours behind us, so she is on the telephone at odd moments – and I have to confess I find her conversations so rewarding that I have found myself loitering in the hall, eavesdropping, instead of getting on with the delivery of the full English to our children.

July

When the telephone rang at 9 a.m. on Saturday, we were all still in bed, so I hurtled downstairs to the hall before it rang off. A transatlantic voice identified himself as the producer boyfriend, Jake. 'I just called to say goodnight to Antonia before I go to sleep,' said Jake, even though it was morning on Exmoor.

So I got Antonia up and she came down in her adorable cashmere pyjamas, sparked up a cigarette and sat chatting to Jake, while I cleared the children's cereal bowls and started offering eggs and bacon. After half an hour, Antonia joined us.

'How's Jake?' I asked.

'Well, he's been to see his psychic. And she says that he needs to worry less and that there are issues around our boundaries.'

'Oh yes?' I said, scraping sodden Shreddies into dog bowls as if no one in West Somerset would ever be without their pet psychic.

'Yeah,' said Antonia. 'He sneaks in by her back door because he doesn't want anyone knowing.

He'd been to breakfast at Urth, that's U-R-T-H, by the way, the organic café where the bacon and sausages are 100 per cent lean turkey, and then he went to Hands On, this spa place, to see if he could find this particular orange-blossom-scented candle I'm crazy about.'

'Orange-blossom-scented candle?' I repeated softly, chiselling fried egg off the hotplate with a carving knife.

'Yeah. Isn't that sweet? He wants the one I always light when I'm in Beverly Hills. So, anyway, he gets the candle and then he swings by the gym for his two-hour workout, and then he grabs a lightly seared tuna wrap for his lunch . . .'

'Lightly seared tuna wrap . . . how lovely,' I murmur, unloading the dishwasher for the seventh time in twelve hours. 'Carry on telling me while we get ready. Right, children. How about a walk?'

So we route-march the children up the hill to the top of the farm, by dint of offering each child one Kit Kat Kube per two fields climbed, until we reach the summit at 1,400 ft. 'Wow,' says Antonia, gratifyingly, as I point out Dunkery Beacon, the highest point on Exmoor, and gesture towards the moorland encircling our river valley. I like this moment, because this panorama, with its plump green valleys and flash of the Bristol Channel, makes even the towniest of philistines catch their breath.

'Wow,' she says again. 'There's nothing for miles. It's really beautiful. I can't wait to tell Jake.'

So, when Jake calls the next morning to say goodnight, she tells him at length all about our long 'hike' with two dogs and five children in the 'wilderness' and cooking on the 'sixty-year- old range'.

Then she comes through to my dark Exmoor kitchen, where I am all ears, awaiting the latest bulletin from sunny Beverly Hills. 'I've told him all about this part of the West Country and Jake can't wait to visit,' she says. 'Actually, he thinks we should move here, for a while,' she continues, as I begin to wonder whether they are both as mad as snakes or whether they are, in fact, having me on. 'But he's gonna have to check with his psychic first.'

july

When my last batch of house guests left on Tuesday, they were understandably a little wary. 'So what are you going to say about us?' they demanded over breakfast – no doubt recalling my faithful transcriptions of Antonia's telephone conversations, which had appeared verbatim in my newspaper column the week before.

'Actually, you've got nothing to worry about,' I replied. 'You've all left me woefully short of copy. The larder's bare – unless I go public with Jim's really remarkable snoring, which I might.'

It would be a shame not to, because I have over several years conducted first-hand research into Jim's snoring (our bedroom is adjacent to the 'main' guest bedroom). Moreover, I'd gone to the trouble of doing further homework into the subject by innocently bringing it up during the course of a long walk on the moor with his wife, Julie.

Well, I hit the jackpot because Julie said that Jim not only snored (well, I could have told her that) but also insisted on having a final cup of coffee just before turning in. 'It's a habit,' she said. So, moments before he heads up the wooden stairs to Bedfordshire, he makes himself a treacly cup of nerve-jangling Nescafé.

This, apparently (and I have, of course, to rely on her evidence), ensures that his already world-beating snoring is interspersed with many long hours of tossing, turning, impatient sighs about the non-appearance of the sandman, and – at this point, I was almost shrieking with disbelief – switching on his bedside light. To read, forsooth!

Well, I could hardly believe my ears, but it was a jolly instructive conversation to have, because it made me realize what a horrible bed-Nazi I have become.

While Julie lies patiently alongside her honking, whiffling husband, and still rises up singing, I am the reverse. If my husband makes the slightest noise as he inhales or exhales, I can't help making the same frowning tut of irritation I emit if a close family member is eating cereal, chewing gum or clacking a sweet around their mouth in my presence.

I operate a policy of zero tolerance, especially when I am trying to sleep, which I justify by telling my long-suffering family that I am acutely 'noise sensitive'. So I have been known to prod my husband awake to accuse him of 'breathing'. (He turns over like a lamb, muttering his apologies.)

Hitherto, I had persuaded myself that my husband would prefer me to tell him than resent him for keeping me awake. But now I can't be so sure. When I think about the fuss I made when he forgot to turn off our electric blanket this Easter, so I woke up in a flop sweat in the early hours, thinking the house was burning down . . . I blush.

The truth is, I now realize, that the test of an accommodating marriage is not loving each other's friends and families as one's own, making sacrifices for each other's careers or agreeing about education. It is sharing a bedroom.

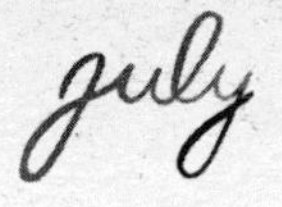

It must be vanishingly rare to find two people who always agree on such issues of global concern: duvet versus blankets? Window open or shut? Heating on or off? As Leonard Woolf (I think) said, the secret of a happy marriage is to share a roof, but not a ceiling.

So it is a tribute to my husband that in the winter we lie with our noses poking over the sheets in a bedroom so cold we can see our own nostril breath at the break of day, when, given any choice, he would lie on a toasty electric blanket, next to a roaring radiator, with the window sealed tightly shut.

I take my hat off to him and to Julie, for not merely learning to live with the irritating nocturnal habits of their spouses, but doing so with the sort of Christian forbearance that has always eluded me.

July

Down on Exmoor, where I am permanently ravenous, I am coming to terms with the horrid reality with which so many of my friends, aged thirty-five and beyond, are already grappling. If we eat 'normally', our jeans, shall we say, do not exactly hang off our bony frames. As forty is the new twenty, one cannot be seen to give in to middle-age spread.

There seem to be two approaches to the problem.

The first is to spend all hours in the gym, sweating off the few calories you have permitted to pass your panting lips. The second is to starve. One dear friend maintains her slender form by pecking on flaxseed in the morning and fruit for lunch, and then gorging on a small salad in the evening after her three boys (who, she says, have never seen her eat) are in bed.

I know another woman who has Diet Coke for breakfast and lunch, staves off hunger pangs with Extra sugar-free gum, and eats for the first and only time in the day with her children at teatime. In her case, her husband never sees her eat (apart from a little something at weekends).

It is now accepted that serving any form of carbohydrate at a social function is an 'aggressive act'. Most people I know are duly on the Atkins or South Beach diets, or following M. Montignac and subsisting on claret, filet mignon and dark chocolate. Now, it is all very well (and jolly dull) us adults being on permadiets, eliminating wheat, dairy and rice, and living on broccoli juice. But we seem to expect our children to have a 'healthy approach' to food despite the evidence before them that we, the parents, have gone completely tonto.

I recently witnessed a furious row between an otherwise reasonably sane couple over their son's consumption of a slice of treacle tart at my lunch table, which resulted in an escalating conflict over the range of raw wholefoods the five-year-old would have to eat at teatime to compensate: seven grapes, two slices of apple and at least four carrot batons.

For the past ten days, though, we have been almost carb-free, thanks to a visiting friend, Fiona. (The only hiccup in an otherwise harmonious week was when she served bolognese sauce on a bed of shredded cabbage instead of pasta, and Oliver sobbed for two hours.)

So faddy has arrived, even in wild and woolly Somerset. We were asked out to lunch this week. 'What diet are you doing?' asked Charlotte (they were on South Beach) when she telephoned to invite us to Bampton. 'The no-carbs,' I replied. When we arrived, there was a huge dish of lasagne, glossy with bechamel and rich with chicken livers, bubbling from the Aga, for children and non-dieting adults. For the dieting adults there was salmon and a watercress salad. We all declined wine.

'I don't understand,' said Charlotte's handsomely upholstered husband, Gerard, as he wolfed his salmon in one gulp, like Timmy the dog in the Famous Five with a dish of ice-cream. 'We're not drinking. We're not even eating. What on earth are we all doing here having lunch together?'

Thank God for that. We decided the salmon had been the perfect starter, dug into the lasagne and cracked open some delicious Bordeaux, and proceeded to have a perfectly lovely lunchtime like

we all used to before the new diet revolution.
To do otherwise would have been, as we all agreed,
an aggressive act.

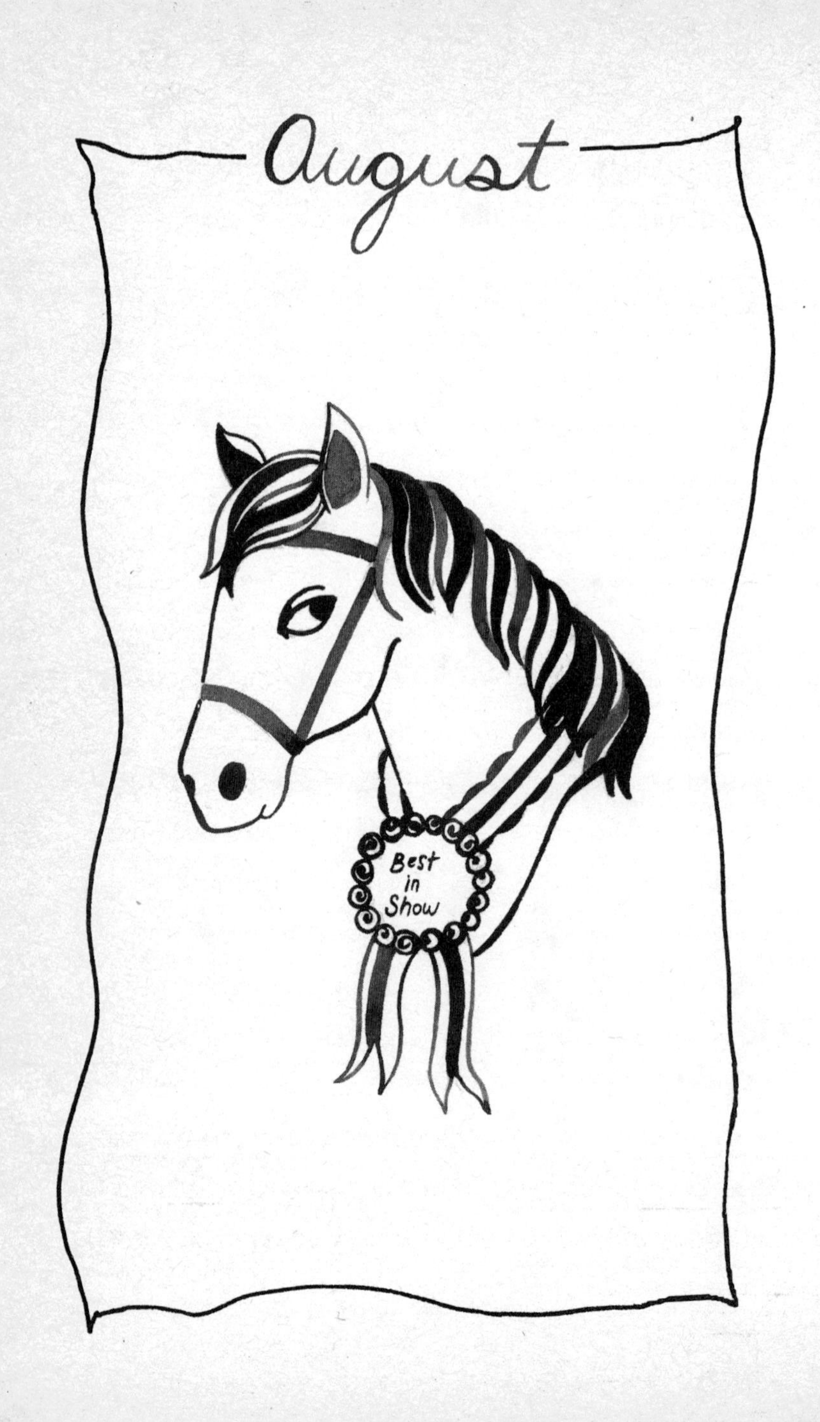
August
Best in Show

August

Ah, the bliss of not having the school run is my first though as I awake. This glorious lassitude lasts a second, because my next thought is the weather. If I can see golden sunlight on green leaves, I leap out of bed in a panic and run outside.

I muck out the stables, then go down to the meadow, where Bobby and Ella are grazing, fatly. Just to make this a proper holiday, a real rest, I am (brave sigh) in charge of twelve people (six children), two dogs (one on heat), one pony and a horse – and the horse is an albino mare that dislikes having factor-sixty sunblock applied to her nostril area even more than my children do.

I tend to think that things will be a piece of cake, so when Charlotte (she of Bampton lasagne lunch) sweetly offered to lend us Bobby when my daughter was at the height of her 'pony phase' this spring, I whinnied for joy. When Charlotte offered us Ella too, I neighed even more excitedly, because then it would be like the Pony Club (only a lot more fun, obviously). So when we got down here I cleared the stables and went to Exmoor Farm Supplies for bedding, buckets, hay-nets and hoof-picks, in time for Charlotte and her daughter, Lettie, to ride our new charges over from Bampton.

'Bobby head-butts, so don't put your face down when you're tacking up,' advised Charlotte over a quick cup of tea and rock cake, before bolting off to Cornwall. 'And he likes to tread on your feet,' added Lettie, 'so wear boots.'

'Ella's a sweetie, though,' continued Charlotte, fondly. 'The children should be on her by the end of the fortnight. She's fast, so just keep contact with her mouth and sit tight and you'll be fine.'

Throughout this conversation, I nodded sagely – in order, of course, to give the impression that I learnt to ride, like Dick Francis, before I could walk, and was only happy when astride eighteen hands of rippling horseflesh. I was relying, basically, on my sensible friend Fiona to tell us all what to do, which she did. But after only ten days of being an unpaid stable-hand, groom and riding instructor (as well as cook), Fiona very selfishly went on a sailing holiday with her children to Salcombe and left me on my own. I had a mobile number for Charlotte, but didn't want her to know that I was lacking in 'horse sense'. So I had to fall back on my father's old copy of *A Handbook for Horse Owners* by Lt Col M. F. McTaggart, DSO, in its fifth printing in 1951. This turned out to be a very useful tool, but something of a double-edged sword.

'Remember a groom cannot groom a horse without perspiring over it,' dictates the Lt Col. 'Rules for grooming routine: 7 a.m., stable should be opened and cleaned out; horses' feet picked, and mane and tail brushed . . .'

And so on, hour by hour, until 8 p.m., and the 'Final look round and hay-up'.

Clearly, I have failed to grasp that having a horse is a full-time job. I feel rather relieved that my grandfather is not here to witness my fumblings with girths and so on. He once thrashed my father after he, my father, had replied, in answer to a gruff demand, that yes, he had 'seen' his horse Simon one morning. In fact, he had seen him only through the bathroom window and hadn't spent the requisite half-hour rubbing his withers and sponging his dock, or whatever, which is what my grandfather clearly meant, as I now know from my handbook.

But I still couldn't find anything in it to help me with Ella, who tends to gallop very fast when I ride her, often by hedges and under hanging branches. 'The gallop is not a pace at which those not engaged at racing ought to proceed,' is all the Lt Col says. 'It is therefore beyond the scope of this book.'

Nor does he explain why sweet Ella drags her lips away from her teeth and eyeballs me when I try to put her bridle on. Nor why darling Bobby, for that matter, nips and tumbles children over his neck into nettles.

Fiona keeps saying that I have an 'electric bum', which sounds like the new single from Kylie. I can't find ‘electric bum’ or indeed ‘horse whisperer’ in the index, but came across a withering explanation for Ella’s startling turns of speed.

Any equine bad habits are the fault of the rider, who has failed to have his mount under ‘moral control’, says the Lt Col, the magisterial author of *Mount and Man* and *Stable and Saddle*, and who am I to contradict him?

I guessed something was up on Day One. ‘What time will you ring tomorrow?’ asked my eldest son in a small voice over the telephone. He and his sister were at what I had been calling ‘pony camp’ for a much-anticipated few days last week. I had waxed on about mucking out and trying jumps, as Labradors entwined about their jodhpured legs and Mrs D, the riding instructress and all-round mother figure, got them to join in. My daughter, nine, was lit up at the prospect and had packed her suitcase days before. My son was more suspicious.

When I went to pick them up from the stables on Day Three, they were sitting in complete silence waiting to be served their crumble, which Mrs D was dishing up in the kitchen. There were teenage stable-girls, some teenagers and Mr D, but no children their age. I picked my way towards where they were sitting, too cowed to move. As I gave my son's shoulder a pat (I could tell this was a house where horses and dogs came first, but where children were never to be fussed over), his eyes filled with tears. 'Can't we just go now?' he begged. I looked over at my daughter to see whether his tears were mummy manipulation, but she gave only a sorrowing look of numb resignation that I recognized from somewhere.

While even younger than them, in the heady first years of Britain becoming a part of Europe, my brother and I were sent to a summer camp. It was called Pinksterblom, a name you could never forget because it was written in sinister letters over an arch at the camp's entrance. The camp was near a seaside town called Sluys ('sluice') in Holland and was surrounded by polders and long, rough grasses. It was set up as a perk for Eurocrats, who could send their lucky, lucky children there for virtually nothing during the long *vacances*.

We went by coach from Brussels, me faint with excitement because this was the first time I had been away from home, and in my kit-bag I had my very own, brand-new sleeping-bag, orange plastic plate, cup, knife and fork, and soap in its own special dish. I had scoffed airily when, as she kissed us goodbye, my mother said that if we really hated it we could come home. My elder brother sat next to me on the bus and gazed thoughtfully out of the window.

When we arrived at the camp, we were told which tent to go to. There were eight other children in mine, packed in like sardines. They were all Dutch. There was a strong smell of pee. I laid out my new sleeping-bag, then proceeded, as per instructions, to the dining area, taking with me my plate, cup, knife and fork. We all sat at long trestle tables. I couldn't see my brother anywhere.

During a week of continuous rain, we ate sugar sandwiches and boiled potatoes, washed down with sour milk, or sour milk with sugar. If we wanted to go to the camp's one loo, we had to find our monitor and ask him for paper, a commodity with which he was most sparing.

As it was so wet, we spent our days going on walks or peeling potatoes in monkish silence because my brother and I spoke no Dutch apart from the Dutch for sour milk and sour milk with sugar.

At the weekend, my father arrived. I don't think I've ever been so pleased to see anyone. We explained in a calm and unemotional way that Pinksterblom wouldn't do. We told him about everyone peeing in the tent, the dreadful food, the unspeakable loo, that no one had spoken a word to us all week.

'Please, Dada,' we begged, as he looked at his watch, calculating whether he'd be back in Brussels in time for dinner. 'We really can't take it. Please let us come home with you.'

August

My brother says that as Dada pulled away we ran after the car, sobbing. I don't remember that. All I remember is that we tried to use our Get Out of Jail Free cards, the ones our mother always gave us along with our goodbye kisses, and we couldn't. This is why my children know they can always use theirs. I'll be the first to hoick them out of French schools, or pony camp, or boarding school if it comes to that, at the merest tremble in the voice, because I remember.

'Hey, Dada,' I asked, having filled him in on pony camp this week. 'Why didn't you let us come back to Brussels with you that time?' My father, who – apart from that one dereliction – can do no wrong, did not look shifty in the least.

'Because you hadn't done the second week, of course,' he replied.

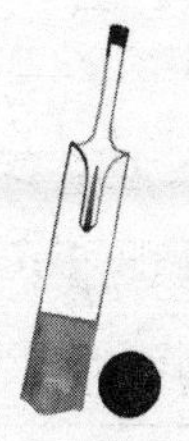

August

It's Tuesday, it's 3 p.m. and therefore it's Changeover Time in our remote Somerset fastness, where a constant stream of guests from London has been booked in case the grown-ups get bored and whiny. On Changeover Day, the daddy nobly lays aside his newspaper and takes the children down to splash for a while in the Exe river, while the mummy bustles round packing.

I hover, saying helpful things like: 'Don't forget all your funny goat's-milk stuff in the fridge – my children are unfashionably tolerant to cow's milk!' or 'I couldn't help noticing all your washbags are still in the bathroom!' and 'Leave the sheets, I'm sure they can live to fight another day!'

Then I prepare my M4 survival pack: a bar of what my grandmother used to call 'motoring chocolate' and foil-wrapped sausages, still warm from the Aga, which I press into the departing mummy's hand with my domestic-goddess face on.

As I wave them off, graciously accepting thanks for my farmhouse hospitality, I can usually hear the next people-mover, filled with whey-faced

London children, bumping up the drive.

The next lot of friends will unfurl themselves, shake off the sweet wrappers, and begin to marvel at our hidden valley, our burbling river, bracken-clad hillsides, barns and other rustic amenities.

'This is paradise!' they exclaim. 'I can't think how you drag yourselves back to London.'

If it's not raining, we have tea in the garden – homemade scones, which I urge everyone to have with butter and clotted cream. It's at about this point – as I am setting the table for children's high tea – that new arrivals can start talking in a strange way. For example, Sam.

'Another scone, Sam, to go with your clotted cream?' I asked Sam, a television journalist, who had just arrived.

'Rather!' roared Sam, reaching for the butter first, before generously adding cream. 'I must say, they're topping.' I should explain that Sam is a hardened war correspondent who made his name reporting bloodcurdling African atrocities. Yes, there's something about the ancestral Johnson pridelands that brings out the Blyton in even the most metropolitan of Somerset visitors.

'So the children can just roam around?' Sam went on, gazing around the valley with shining eyes. 'It's completely safe?'

I nodded.

'Isn't that super,' Sam said, dreamily, as he pushed a scone wobbling with cream and jam into his jaws. 'Just as it should be. A proper childhood.'

And, as my children go about in their top-to-toe Mini-Boden, and refuse my suggestions that they go off to 'make camps' down by the river, I can quite see Sam's point.

Appearances do seem to suggest that I am fulfilling the fantasy of all the middle-class parents, which is to provide the childhood we all read about in *Five Go Off in a Caravan.*

But appearances can be deceptive.

In fact, I am considering calling for a cultural reappraisal of Enid Blyton, because I think her oeuvre is fundamentally misunderstood.

I have been rereading *Five Go to Demon's Rocks,*

which I found on a bookshelf in my daughter's room, and it is, of course, as ripping as I remember.

Might I just point out, though, that Uncle Quentin and Aunt Fanny make it quite clear that the Famous Five are outstaying their welcome in Kirrin Cottage, and pack the team off to a lighthouse with a little boy called Tinker.

In *Five Fall into Adventure*, the Famous Five come to stay just as Uncle Q and Aunt F are off to Spain, and are thus left home alone at Kirrin Cottage. ('If we don't go tomorrow all our arrangements will be upset,' Aunt Fanny explains.)

And in *Five Go Off in a Caravan*, George suggests that they scarper, with the explanation: 'I bet the grown-ups will be glad to be rid of us. They always think the summer hols are too long.'

So, while I am all for lashings of fresh air and independence, I contest that this is not all the sainted Enid reveals about the 'proper' English childhood.

Blyton's narrative action is driven by parental reluctance to be with their own children (q.v. the St Clare's and Mallory Towers series), leaving them blissfully free to determine how they spend their time.

To that extent, I realize, my own poor children could not be more constrained. I am forcing them to spend sixty-five days (my son is ticking them off, like a prisoner in solitary confinement) with me on Exmoor.

They are, frankly, fed up. When I fell into bed last night, exhausted, my ten-year-old son had left a note on my pillow.

How sweet, how literary, I thrilled, as I picked it up. 'The Country is Pants. London Rocks,' it said.

Given any choice, of course, my son would not be hiking off to Demon's Rocks with Tinker. It would be straight back to topping Notting Hill with Sam, in a nice warm car, and what Darrell Rivers of Mallory Towers would doubtless call the 'motoring chocolate'.

August

So, Bobby (the pony) and Ella (the albino mare) are back in Bampton with Lettice and Charlotte and we have moved further west, to Cornwall, where we are haunting the pasty parlours of Tintagel, clotted-cream ice-cream stands, and surf shacks selling board shorts in splashy, tropical colourways.

I love Cornwall. The cliffs and coastal paths. Bodmin Moor. Godrevy lighthouse. Thunder-and-lightning pudding. The crashing surf. And, above all, the fact that everyone on this stretch of the coast is dressed identically for most of the time, which solves the summer problem of female grooming in the simplest way imaginable. I have always been concerned about what is expected of mothers past thirty in the grooming department. This uncertainty started when I lived in Belgium and went for an eyelash tint in one of the city's numerous *salons de beauté*. I had made the appointment over the telephone and distinctly said 'lash tint' in my best French to the receptionist.

I was ushered into the treatment room and was invited to repose myself on the divan. I lay with my eyes shut and began to feel pleasantly drowsy, the inevitable consequence of lying down in the middle of the day and submitting to the tender ministrations of a young woman in a white coat.

I became aware, despite my torpid state, of the beautician leaning over me and peering closely at my face. I could feel her warm breath on my cheek. I lay there for what seemed like ages, wondering what she was doing.

'*Madame est ici*,' she inquired hesitantly, when at last I opened my eyes and looked into hers, '*pour le duvet?*' As I had no idea what she meant, I couldn't say, rather stiffly, that I most certainly was not, and merely repeated my desire to have my eyelashes dyed.

Then she ran a light finger over my upper lip, and I realized that she was referring to the moustache (and in some cases beard) that adorns women past a certain age. The beautician explained that in Belgium all women have their duvets removed at the first sign of downiness. '*C'est normale*,' said the beautician, as she continued to contemplate my upper lip with a hungry look.

I had my lash tint and left, feeling thoughtful. What if she'd seen my legs, I mused anxiously? And why were ferally hairy armpits *normale* – even erotic – in the Francophone world but a fine dusting of adorable baby-blonde hairs on the upper lip unacceptable?

I am aware, of course, that many women simply get on with it, get their roots done, their waxing over with, before they dare bare any flesh at all in summer. I am not among them. In my view, blonde hair does not count and is only noticeable in any case to its owner, a belief that remains unshaken despite the visibility of my duvet to a keen-eyed Belgian beautician.

But when we were on Exmoor last week, we went swimming in the Barle. I had unfortunately left the swimming bag carefully by the car before driving off to the moor, so we were garbed in an assortment of pants and T-shirts that clung in ghastly fashion to our – for want of an even more horrible expression – 'bits and bobs'. I was in vest and knickers, but Amanda went swimming in T-shirt, pants and combat trousers, because, as she explained, her pants were translucently white.

So imagine my joy when I get here to Cornwall and realize that I can cast my grooming anxieties to the Atlantic winds and salt spray.

My new uniform extends from the neck to the ankles, is made of water- and sunproof hi-tech neoprene. I have always been suspicious when Muslim women laud the freedom and anonymity afforded by the veil, but now I am converted to my new, infinitely covetable Cornish burqa.

My new wetsuit, of course. If I could, I'd sleep in mine.

In Cornwall, I found it strangely easy to decline my husband's daily offers to 'jump in the car' and zoom off to see some historic house 'only a couple of hours away', even those that he claimed held fine tombs of his family's medieval ancestors. In the end we managed one, Lanhydrock House – just outside Bodmin – where you follow a sequent tour of fifty or so rooms, as directed by kindly National Trust guides and arrows.

In Room 2 (the Butler's Pantry, I think) I realized that we were exclusively shunting along the circuit with none other than Richard and Judy off the telly and their teenage son. So celebrity-struck am I that I was quite overcome by their proximity and quite failed to take in the finer points of the family portraits, while Richard and Judy and their son quietly absorbed the high Victorian atmosphere with a total lack of self-consciousness.

I think we finally parted company in Her Ladyship's Boudoir (Room 34), so I was able to hiss to my husband – who evidently wouldn't recognize a prime-time presenter even if he was wedged up against a brace of them in a game larder – who those nice people who had smiled at our children were. We both thought what a lovely, lovely family. A super couple.

On Exmoor, though, I am a persistent attender of dog and flower shows, fêtes, and the county shows that pop up on grassy hillsides and village greens throughout the summer, as one is when living in the depths of a river valley without television.

Anyway, Ludo, who needs the Notting Hill Carnival when you can go to the Dulverton Scuffle? The lanes for miles around are clogged with trailers carrying ancient Land Rovers and off-roaders, making their way to the scuffle, which is a bit like the Paris–Dakar rally, only there's no desert and the cars go round and round a field in a sea of mud at ten miles an hour, crashing into each other.

Needless to say, this diesel- and testosterone-fuelled jolly was enjoyed by all except the barrister who had just got off the train from London. He thought he was going to have a lovely, quiet Saturday smelling the newly mown hay and watching the swallows, then perhaps going on a nature ramble with his sons. At one point he sank down on to a bank, overpowered by noise and fumes and spattered with the mud thrown up by spinning tyres. 'Sorry, Edward,' our hostess said. 'But this is what passes for entertainment in North Devon.'

Last Monday's *fête champêtre* – a fifty-eighth annual 'revel' and gymkhana in a village on the edge of the moor – was even more high-toned, even though on paper it was the usual fayre: skittles, produce, jumble, tea tent.

As I watched children being prepared for the mounted fancy-dress competition in Ring 1, though, I became aware of an even more enchanting sideshow. Gosh, the British know how to do fancy dress, I was thinking, as I admired a small gaucho astride a pony, its mane entangled with roses; a Winnie-the-Pooh atop Eeyore; a pair of turbaned Talibans; a punk pony ridden by a Mohawked five-year-old, spray-painted slogans on its flanks. What imagination!

But then the most popular sideshow of the whole revel wandered on to the greensward in front of me.

She was wearing a miniskirt with a Hawaiian print, which revealed about a yard of toned brown withers and very pretty fetlocks that disappeared into designer lace-up wellies. This ensemble (think yummy mummy meets *Straw Dogs*) was saved from being mortally provocative by the accessory she held in her arms, a tow-headed, squirming toddler.

As I had been feeling the wind, I had just purchased a long coat for a pound in the jumble sale; this I was wearing, with a towel I had found in the boot of the car as a scarf. As I was attracting very little attention, to say the least, I was even more aware of this other mother's electric progress around the revel.

The man standing next to me was similarly enthralled. 'She has just been at the skittles,' he informed me. 'What a fine filly! Great fun, eh?' Then my husband came up to where we were watching the gymkhana. 'Do you think we could persuade her to compete in the bending race?' he asked, eyeing the briefness of her skirt.

Oh yes, great fun! 'I think they should forget

about the dogs and the ponies and the children and just put the mummies into the ring,' observed my husband most generously, as we drove home. 'I'd definitely give you a rosette for second best in show.'

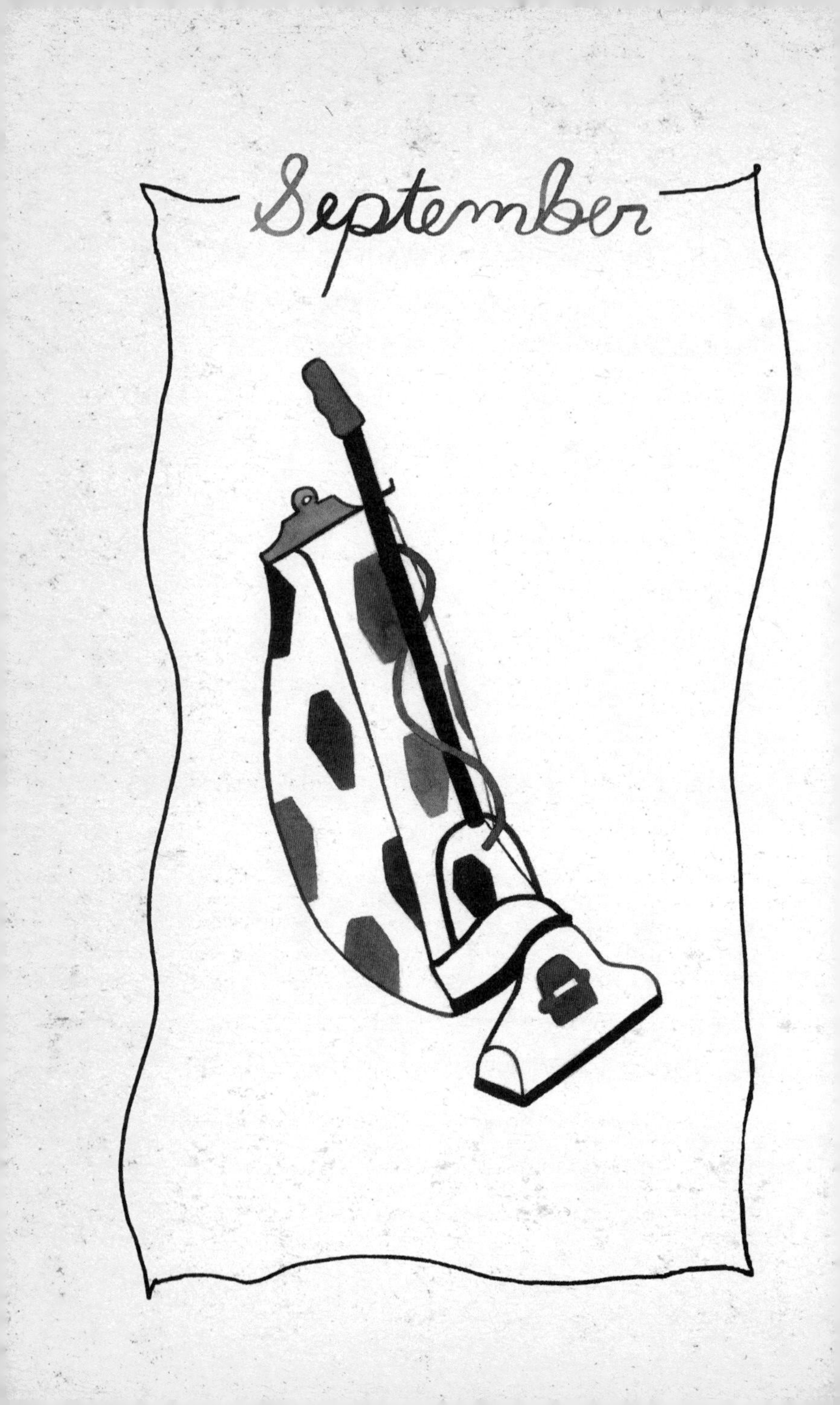
September

September

Having implied in July's entries that Exmoor folk are all on various faddy diets, I am going to retract this insult.

Actually, we don't need to be on diets. I now realize that merely being in the countryside without help (of which more later!) is such a workout that we burn off thousands of calories a day 'just staying alive', as my husband puts it.

The holidays are drawing to an end, I feel fit as a fiddle and I don't even hunt, which is what people do round here, of course, instead of going to the gym. My arms are toned from hauling bundles of wet sheets from the washing machine to the line and from vacuuming and sweeping (often on hands and knees with dustpan and brush). My hands are raw from rinsing leeks under ice-cold taps and scrubbing potatoes, and my hair a tangled mat.

As I write this, I have sent my husband, children and sainted mother-in-law down to the river with the dog so I can make lunch. I have just an hour before our last summer guests arrive, en route to Clovelly, during which time I must lay the table, wash bed-linen and tidy the house.

To begin with, it is always rather a novelty, pegging out washing and turning out bedrooms, and so on. But pretty soon, you know, the *hausfrau* sense of satisfaction wears off and the mealtimes come round so fast they run into each other. No sooner is breakfast over than I have to think about lunch and, yesterday, my mother-in-law was just finishing a cup of tea when my husband put her cocktail (a lethal vermouth-based concoction known only as 'mother's drink') in her free hand.

Sometimes, the unrelenting domesticity – aerobic though it is – makes me feel like the Nancy Mitford heroine who complains, after she has got married, that it was all rather a shock to 'One'.

September

After hunting, Linda Radlett says, one was made to rest for hours and was given eggs for tea, but after a morning's housework – which is, as Linda points out, just as exhausting – 'One is expected to carry on as if nothing has happened.'

I tried carrying on as if nothing had happened for a while but this week decided to use a technique we called, as children, 'brave sighing'.

Brave sighing – passed down the female line – is the way mothers wordlessly indicate a state of domestic martyrdom. As one enters a room and gathers up the coffee cups, one exhales audibly.

Ditto as you clear the lunch table, wander about wiping with a damp cloth, or unload the dishwasher for the third time that day.

Now, the only downside of brave sighing is that men, in my experience, tend to assume from your palpable mood that you are having a feminine moment, as if nothing else could possibly explain your strange demeanour. And then they seek to have their suspicions confirmed.

'Of course I'm not pre-menstrual!' I screamed at

my husband, when he made his infuriating suggestion, gripping the Aga rail for strength (and wondering, as I reviewed the date, whether he was right). 'It's just that I hate [a catch in the voice works well here] asking for help, that's all.'

'Of course you do, and you shouldn't have to,' my husband responded in soothing tones. 'Would you like me to do some Hoovering?'

'Yes please,' I said, with a grateful look.

Instead of doing the floors, though, he decided that the house was in urgent need of 'cobwebbing'.

So he was cobwebbing cornices when our six-year-old found him. Oliver stood there, appalled. 'Daddy! What are you doing?' he wailed, at the piteous sight of his father with a 1600-watt Hoover PurePower. 'Why is Mummy making you do all her work?'

September

I return to London after six lovely but long weeks in Cornwall and Somerset, in order to try to resume work and to prepare my children for school.

So why am I back, you ask, when I could be eking out an existence of Thesiger-like rusticity in the depths of Exmoor, picking juicy wild blackberries and with only sheep and palmy teenage shepherd boys for company?

Well, a political crisis has called my husband briefly back *again* to Kenya. I do not especially yearn to spend a hermetic seventh week on my own with the children on Exmoor, particularly as we are upgrading the farm track, which means it is impossible to get in or out of the valley during working hours. And anyway, I reason, it is about time I offloaded the children on to Barbara, our au pair, who has been in residence in our Notting Hill home for the duration of the summer.

Barbara is smart enough to decline my offers to accompany the family when we leave London, you see. My cleaner is even smarter; she has cut a deal whereby I not only pay her when she goes on holiday but I also pay her when I go on holiday, during which time she declines to do the house – i.e., I pay her not to work, for months at a time.

'I so sorry,' says Barbara, shrugging and looking desolate, as I enthusiastically outline plans in early June to spend the whole summer in the West Country, and describe the burbling streams, the bracken-clad hills, the herds of red deer with such passion that I bring tears to my own eyes. 'I love her too, the nature. But I cannot to come. You know I have my [she looks gravely into my eyes] stoddies.'

Barbara takes her 'stoddies' very seriously indeed, as she is required to spend (as I understand it) several hours a day at language school. So any dereliction of what I see as her primary duty, which is to be my constant helpmeet, can be excused by prior obligations to the Home Office.

So I have not seen Barbara for six weeks. At one point over the summer, I rather thought I could use an extra pair of hands, so I contacted an agency in Chard, and it very sent me some details of au pairs, but I put the forms somewhere and forgot them.

When I get back to London, after the traditional six hours behind a caravan on the A303, there is no sign of Barbara, as she has taken advantage of our absence by getting a part-time job over the summer.

In the morning (the children are delighted to see her and immediately start deploying her on what they see as her primary duty, which is to serve them snacks in front of the television), she tells me her good news.

'I am waiting six weeks,' she says, shaking her head, 'and no visa, no visa! I am wanting to go, but no visa, until yesterday! Six weeks, I am in London, stoddying, working, stoddying! And now, I have visa, I am going on holiday, yes?'

Now, I know that I live a life of what must seem like obnoxious privilege, what with houses on Exmoor and in Notting Hill . . . au pair . . . blah-blah . . . cleaner . . . blah-blah-blah . . . endless foreign trips. But I challenge you not to sympathize with me now that, on the very day after I return from the country (having been, I remind you, 'in sole charge' of my own offspring for *weeks*), my au pair announces her plans to depart on a long-haul holiday.

As I unpack and do load after load of laundry, I consider my options, given that my cleaner is also away, on paid leave in India, until October.

Should I hire contract cleaners? A temp? Or should I just accept that playing house and round-the-clock childcare is my lot until my staff resume their posts?

As I get round to my own suitcase, I find the envelope from Just Help in Chard, packed with bumf. I cannot resist casting an eye over the application of a German girl called Birgit, and what a delightful application it is: a four-page handwritten personal statement, in English, accompanied by photographs and excellent references. 'Birgit is familiar with all cleansing works in the household,' writes one past employer, glowingly, from Mainz. 'Dusting, vacuuming, cleaning the bottom and the windows. She carries out these works thoroughly and tidily.'

I have to confess that cheered me up.

September

So here we are again: home, children back at school. In theory, this should be terribly liberating and productive.

In practice, of course, my paid help is all on paid holiday and I am a sitting duck for the office-bound or out-of-area family members and others to treat like a one-woman concierge service, so I am, if anything, even busier with the children back at school than I was when graciously chatelaining on Exmoor.

'Are you in the middle of something?' I am asked, generally mid-morning, when I have ambled in from taking Coco for a walk in Kensington Gardens, double latte in hand, and am making an important decision between an Utterly Nutty Niblet and a Forbidden Fruit from the Thornton's box left over from Sunday lunch ('Behind this mysterious, dark chocolate shell you'll find the succulent taste of raspberries, whipped to a frenzy to create a delicate mousse', etc.). 'Not really,' I confess, 'although I should get my head down reasonably soon. What is it?'

At this point, your dear caller will begin to explain that it's frightfully inconvenient (for you, that is) and that his car has been towed away and is residing in the car pound, how the key can be picked up from his cleaning lady south of the river, and so on, and he knows it's a lot to ask, but because you aren't at work, you are the only person available, and if you are really pushed for time, you can (he generously offers) take a taxi.

I've also noticed that if someone leaves London this automatically disables their mobile telephone. I get frequent calls from people telling me they've forgotten to cancel the newspapers/milk/doctor's appointment, or have left their car on a meter, or something. If you ask why they don't make the call/move the car themselves, they reply, somewhat incredulously: 'Because I'm not in London, silly!'

Clearly, this is all my fault. I am somehow failing

to convey the impression that my home life is even more hectic than any office existence. If I did, I might somehow discourage those frequent calls from people who ring up to try to make their problem my problem, a protocol that is not confined to office hours and weekdays, as I was reminded once again last week.

At 8 p.m. last Friday, Sally called to ask if I could kindly supply some maths homework, a task that involved: 1) photocopying pages of sums from a textbook; and 2) faxing them. In deeply apologetic tones, I said I couldn't really help because, even though I worked from home, we did not have a so-called home-office.

I then added, as a clincher, that we were already late for a dinner party.

Sally demolished my excuses as if they were immaterial. 'I know – isn't it a bore? But you'll just have to go out and find a photocopier in a newsagents, somehow, then borrow a friend's fax,' she purred, in tones of sympathetic finality. 'We're in Wiltshire, you see.'

September

We took the children to France last weekend. We hadn't booked anywhere or planned anything, but it just seemed like a good thing to do at the *fin de saison*. But weren't we mad to take the car, friends queried. Wouldn't we end up spending most of the weekend on the *aller* and the *retour*, no matter what we did?

My answer to that is as follows. One, my husband likes nothing more than spending long hours in a car. Two, he is not compelled to subject every decision he takes to complex formulae. But I evaluate clothes by dividing their cost by the number of times worn or washed. I justify spending on inessentials, such as a new T-shirt, by telling myself that I didn't get a parking ticket when my time ran out on a meter. And I assess family trips on an equation of time spent in car, distance travelled and total outlay set against the amount of time we have at our destination, how tired I will feel on Sunday night, and the amount of money we would have saved had we stayed home. It's very scientific. But we both reached, via our separate routes, the same conclusion. We would drive to Le Touquet. It would be lovely.

'We want to hear another language being spoken around us before autumn,' said my husband expansively, 'and eat huge, fattening French meals, and bring back cases of wine.' And to the children he said that this was mummy and daddy's holiday, in which they were included only on sufferance, and that they must put up with visiting churches and spending hours at table in restaurants with a good grace.

Which explains why we ended up spending all of Saturday, our only full day in France, at a water park.

We had left our hotel in Boulogne, after a light breakfast of croissants, brioches, baguette, hot chocolate, fruit, and so on, and made our way down the coast to Etaples. We had lingered in the maritime museum there and the fish market, and then we had taken a leisurely drive to Le Touquet where I played on the wide, sandy beach with the children while my husband spent a pleasant hour rearranging the seats in the back of the van, to avoid having them three abreast and fighting over who got to listen to Busted in the Sony Discman.

Returning from the beach, we stopped to admire a huge structure plonked between the promenade and the seafront, with slides, rides and pools. The children were almost sick with excitement just looking at it. 'Darlings, it's bound to be shut,' I said, as we walked up to the entrance. But it opened at noon. How could I refuse?

Look, I hate water parks as much as the next parent. But I have to admit that Aqualud was fantastic, and not for the reasons you might think. At Aqualud, it was easy to believe that there are no such thing as pan-European health and safety regulations and, I have to say, it gave the place some sizzle.

There were no queues for the slides, because the monitors sat flirting and smoking by the pool, rather than manning the tops of each chute, which were guarded only by red and green lights.

Yes, there were clear signs informing clients that the pregnant and the claustrophobic should pay attention. But it was up to you whether you took your six-year-old down the Black Hole or whether you tried to hack the Twister – a slide so steep that you felt your stomach dropping away and your jowls flapping before you were swirled down a plughole and spat out into a deep pool. It was up to you to decide whether or not your child ate an ice-cream in the water and whether or not you had a beer, or went to the café for a sandwich filled with raw minced beef and raw egg.

It felt a little odd, I suppose, to be inside a steamy water park (and it was definitely a little steamy in the jacuzzis, ahem, if you know what I mean) looking out over a beach where *bon-chic-bon-genre mamans* strolled with blond children in sailor jerseys in the pale sunshine. But I was pleased that I asked how fast one shot down the Twister.

'Of course, the momentum depends on your weight,' said a monitor, as one would expect from a product of the lycée system. '*Vers soixante-cinq kilometres par heure.*' Which means, I calculate, that if I divide distance driven plus time spent in car by my personal velocity in the Twister, the trip to France was *vaut le voyage* after all.

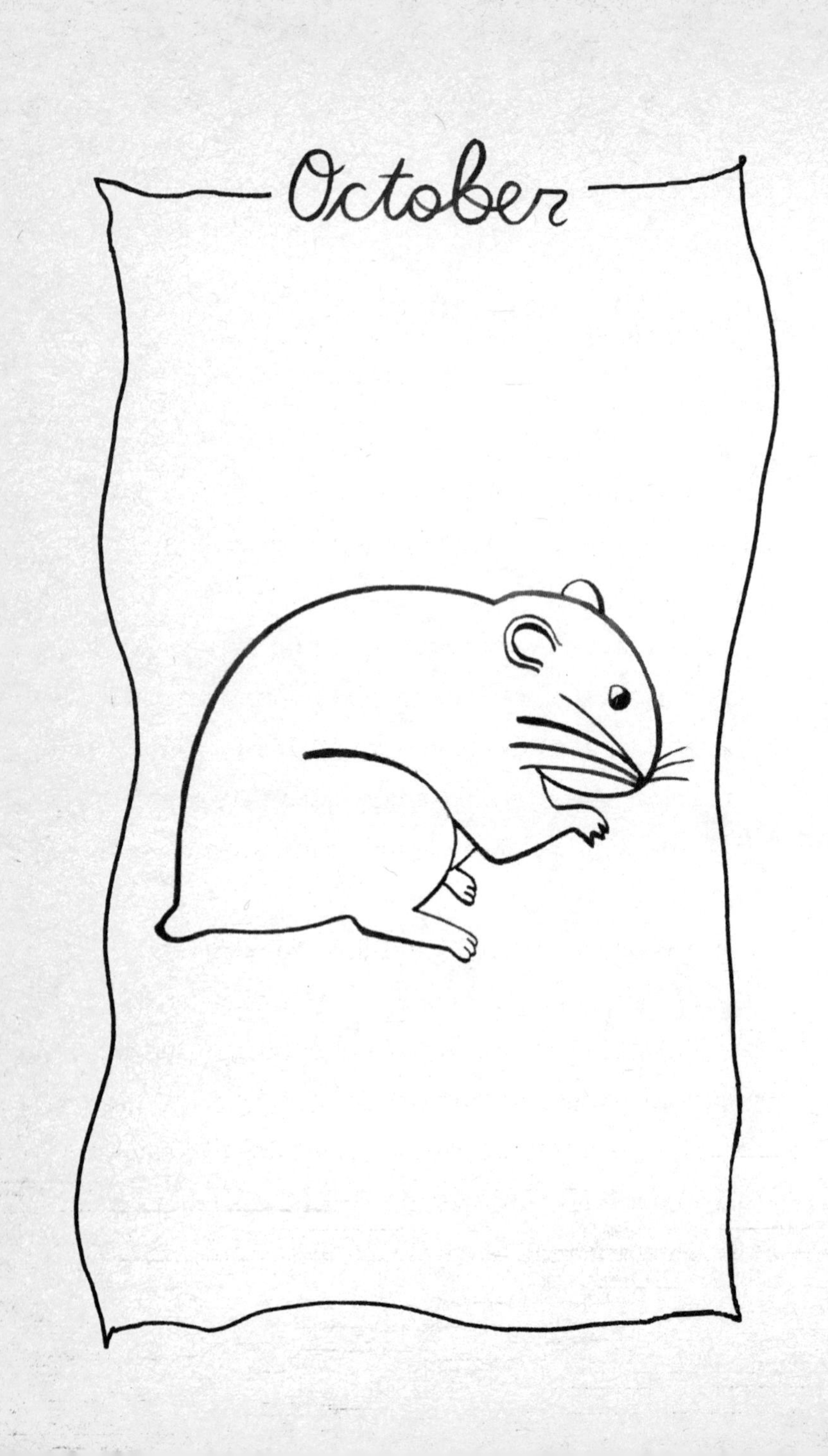
October

October

'So, darling,' I asked, as I tucked in Oliver on his birthday last Sunday, 'what were the best bits about today?'

I knew this was a high-risk question. This was the child who, when in the Masai Mara during our Once in a Lifetime holiday – and we are talking a tented camp with hot-and-cold running Askari servants, linen sheets and proper ceramic bathrooms – went on safari-strike.

It was only our second morning. To be at the water holes by dawn, campers were woken at 6.30 by an Askari bearing a tray of hot chocolate and bourbon creams. And how exciting is that?

So I was expecting full-dress action and excitement when I made my way over to the children's tent in my pith helmet and full Karen Blixen rig.

My youngest, though, was still in his pyjamas. 'Come on, darling, chop chop, we've got to find the Land Rover now,' I cried, 'or it'll leave without us.'

'I'm not coming,' Oliver said, not looking up from his GameBoy. 'I want to stay here. You can just all –' he added generously – 'go ahead without me.' I didn't even begin to say we had flown thousands of miles, not to mention spent thousands of pounds, to go on game drives because it was too early in the morning and my children are, anyway, immune to such arguments. 'But we might see the lion cubs again or even [I played my trump card] the baby leopard.'

'Not *another* baby leopard,' he groaned, as if in pain. 'We saw one yesterday. An' loads of lion cubs,' he added, accurately, and continued over the next ten days to show much more interest in his GameBoy than game, on the grounds that once you've seen one Thompson's gazelle with its ever wiggly tail you've seen them all.

So you see, I hope, why we approach any occasion likely to exaggerate his expectations with trepidation. They seem to offer such infinite scope for disappointment.

'Come on, let's go and get your present at Hamleys,' my husband offered on Saturday, when the child drifted in from football for a drink (we all knew that it would be fatal to choose his main present without his approval).

'It's all right, Dad,' he said, running out again. 'You can go get it on your own.' So my husband very bravely went out and returned with a huge box containing a James Bond 007 Carrera Go!!! Racetrack, with two cars, an Aston Martin and a Jag, to 'recreate the spectacular car chase in *Die Another Day*'.

So this is how the big day went. He opened his cards and then opened his presents from me, which were all drearily improving, because the only catalogue I had was one from an educational toy company. So he got a tell-the-time watch, a whiteboard to practise the alphabet, a magnetic construction kit and – save the best for last, eh? – a fractions flip-chart.

He was very brave about his presents and then I took him and two friends to catch the 10.50 a.m. performance of the new Rugrats movie (as you can imagine, my husband and I were both fighting to go), after which we all went to Pizza Express. At home after lunch, it took my husband and two other grown men an hour and a half to assemble the *pièce de résistance*, the Go!!! Racetrack, with its sixty-six separate parts. The best moment was when my older son suddenly remembered that Dad also gave him a racetrack for his seventh birthday, which he had used only once. It was still downstairs in the playroom in his box, he added helpfully, as my husband tried to slot a chicane into a flyover joist.

When assembled, the racetrack took up the entire sitting-room floor and was a great hit with the three men, who spent ages recreating the car chase from *Die Another Day*, while the birthday boy played in the garden with his new football.

At teatime, I produced the chocolate-mousse cake that I had made the day before. It had set into a claggy dark disc. After he'd blown out the candles, I had to help cut the first slice. 'What did you wish?' asked his sister, as we all nibbled away at the dense slab. 'For a different cake,' he whispered.

'So, darling, what were the best bits about today?' I asked. Was it the presents, the movie, the racetrack?

'Nothing really,' he answered, his lower lip trembling with self-pity.

'I know,' I said, sympathetically, 'birthdays are always a terrible let-down, I'm afraid. It's just something you get used to.' And I gave him a last kiss.

I meet my friend Helen, the corporate wife, for a girly lunch at Nicole Farhi in Westbourne Grove, in order to catch up on key social trends I have missed and to consume my own body-weight in Nicole's famous fried green tomatoes melting with mozzarella.

Helen dutifully filled me in on the latest in childcare (nannies demanding not just nanny-flats but nanny-flats in W11, forsooth!) and the trend for men with working wives to take on more domestic responsibility while they are 'between opportunities' (i.e., laid off from their City jobs).

Apparently, these so-called 'mannies' really swing into action. Without having offices to go to, they recreate one at home. They make spreadsheets for the food shopping, input the teachers' birthdays into their computers and otherwise subject a normally shambolic household to management theory. These mannies are not so much CEOs of the sofa, but i/c all domestic arrangements, so Helen reports, and households run for the first time like Swiss timepieces under their new, McKinsey-style regimes.

'Much as I would dislike having a manny about the house,' I told Helen, ordering a second latte, 'in my experience many husbands I know manage to remote-control their own households without having to be there at all.'

As far as I can see, all it needs is for her indoors to possess a mobile and, hey presto, they have a walking, talking, breathing wife at their beck and call, twenty-four hours a day till death them do part.

I was in Tesco in Brook Green this week. I had done the morning school run, and was planning to have coffee with Clare in Shepherd's Bush and then mosey on home to do a spot of work.

My mobile trilled. 'Where are you?' my husband asked. I explained where I was. 'Well, I need you at home,' he said. 'I need you to log on as me and give me some email addresses from the laptop in the study.' No problem, I said. I'll do it when I get home.

But later in the week he rang me again while I was killing time. I confessed to being in Starbucks (confirming his suspicions that my life is one long punishing round of dog-walking and latte-sipping) then told him of my appointment in ten minutes.

With stunning inevitability, exactly fifteen minutes later – just as I was getting into my stride over a certain itchy mole – my mobile rang. I answered it by hissing: 'I'm with the doctor!'

'I know you're at the doctor's,' my husband said, as if to a small child. 'Very quickly, though. Just remind me what the code is for international directory inquiries.'

The following day, while I was having a swift coffee with Clare, her mobile rang. 'Where are you?' her husband asked from his bank. She revealed her whereabouts. He then instructed her to ring him back in 'no less than fifteen minutes' so they could discuss 'The List'. Clare's face fell.

She told me that 'The List' details the duties that Clare has to perform that day. Clare's beloved calls up to five times a day to monitor progress on, say, the car's MoT or a letter to the school bursar. 'At the end of the day we just slump in front of the TV with a bottle of wine,' Clare said as I fielded a call about a special picture light in Peter Jones that my husband wanted me to buy. 'After so many calls during the course of the day, we have nothing left to say to each other.'

October

According to Clare, this compulsion to control the one who stays at home during working hours is easy to explain. If you are at home, it is clear to the one at the office that you have nothing better to do than run little errands for your husband, who has his hands full devising ever more maddening chores to fill your empty, idling day.

'I happened to be in the King's Road and he rang and asked me to go and look at a chair in George Smith and ring him back,' Clare said. 'I did so and rang him back and he said, that's no good, but don't worry, he thought there was one in this shop in Islington. No wonder they like to think we do nothing all day,' she fretted, 'because they don't want to admit that they keep us entirely busy doing stuff for them.'

October

So this is where we're at, on the my-family-and-other-animals front. The hamster's cage – a funky affair with external tubing, a sort of Pompidou Centre for the rodent in your life – sits desertedly next to Coco's basket. Except for her favourite chewy toy, the basket is as empty as the cage.

Coco has been at boarding-school with a couple who train gun-dogs in the Chilterns (listen, did you think we would train her ourselves?) and returns home tomorrow. As for the hamster . . . well, it has been a long time since Crumpy has been up to any of her favourite tricks, such as going up the blue ladder and entering the tube, which then debouches her in a rather alarming peristalsis-like way through a trapdoor. Or simply lying there, a squashy brown thing in a tunnel, pretending to be asleep.

For Crumpy is in hamster heaven. No, she (he? she?) did not pass away. Crumpy has achieved the single lifetime objective of all hamsters. This fluffy scrap has escaped. The inquest has pointed the finger at Milly's friend Celeste, the last one to play with Crumpy, but not – significantly, we feel – the first to spot that the cage door was open and the hamster gone.

Two days after her break-out, we heard her behind the skirting-board. Then she took up residence in the airing cupboard. Now, she is under the floorboards in a cosy spot just by the Aga. If you lie on your right side, close your left eye and squint through the crack between the Aga's concrete plinth and the floorboards, you can sometimes see her questing pink nose and yellowish front teeth. At night, you can hear Crumpy busily chewing away at some vital gas pipe and crunching away at the Cheerios the children keep pushing down to her.

But my husband and I are not so chuffed. 1) the loud noise of her rootling is very irritating; 2) if Crumpy doesn't make it, there will be a nasty smell; 3) until we recover Crumpy, there is the unanswered question of whether we replace her. I mentioned the dilemma to Antonia. She's the New Yorker who came to stay in the summer and demands instant results.

'Ring the RSPCA, what are you waiting for?' screeched Antonia. 'This is England, you know!' I wait until suppertime. We are eating pasta and trying not to listen to Crumpy munching at the under-floor cables delivering essential household services such as heat and light.

'Apparently,' I say casually, 'the RSPCA will come. It has some sort of service. A sort of hamster hotline,' I conclude, on a hopeful note. This does not go down well.

'Are you mad?' barks my husband, almost drowning the noise of Crumpy's chomping. 'They'll rip up the kitchen. They'll send a SWAT team to tear up the floorboards and we won't be able to stop them. They'll cause thousands of pounds worth of damage. This is England, you know!'

A few days later, I sneak away and call the RSPCA's twenty-four-hour emergency number. I get a very nice man. 'Another hamster under the floorboards – ha ha,' he says. 'We get a lot of these calls. People think we've got the equipment to find him, but we haven't. He'll either come up for food, the same hole he got down,' he predicts sagely, 'or he won't.'

I haven't told Antonia. I doubt, in any case, that she'd come zooming round with a coat hanger and a piece of cheese. 'I'm very bad with small furry animals,' she told me over lunch. 'Once, I took the class guinea pig, Otis, home for the holidays. I had the cage in my room and on the first night I was so excited I played with Otis all night. Boy, we had so much fun, romping around . . .' She trailed off.

'In the morning, Otis was asleep on the floor of his cage, so I went down and my mom said, "How's Otis?" I told her he was asleep. Well, she gave me a look and we went up and – yup! – Otis was dead as a doornail. In rigor. I'd worn him out. It was kinda rough telling all the children in class I'd killed him . . . but that was nothing compared with Fluffy.'

Antonia then told me a story about a cat, illegal substances and an apartment on the twentieth floor on the Upper East Side that *would* have an RSPCA SWAT team hurtling to her door in seconds flat, so I think we'll pass on that.

October

As for Crumpy, all I can say is this, even if it does make me sound like a batty vicar: dear, departed Crumpy is gone. But Crumpy is, in a very real sense, still with us – and that's the hardest part of all.

I have distressing news. Crumpy hamster is, we think, no more. She has passed on. Been gathered to hamster heaven. The silence of the hamster echoes around our basement kitchen even more plangently than the sound of her crunching and chewing. We take solace in knowing, however, that Crumpy's last few days were wild and free.

Still, it was a big consolation going to pick up Coco last weekend. She had been staying with a couple in Buckinghamshire, Mr and Mrs D, the ones who train gun-dogs but also take in the occasional pet and lick 'em into shape.

October

It was up a little lane in the Chilterns. It was a grey, freezing day. As I turned up the lane to drop her off, I had felt like a weepy mother taking her baby to prep school for the first time. I had packed her tuck-box (kibble and treats) and her teddy bear (a fleecy blanket). I held her lead in my hand as we rang the bell.

'Here we are,' I had said, smiling proudly. 'You're late,' barked Mrs D. 'This way.' And she marched ahead to a small, concreted yard where stables had been converted into kennels.

'I'll just get Coco's luggage from the car,' I said. 'By the way, she hasn't had a walk yet today.'

'That's no good, is it?' said Mrs D. 'What do you mean, Coco's luggage? While she's here,' she said grimly, handing me Coco's lead, 'she doesn't need anything.' She then led Coco into a kennel with a concrete floor, empty but for a lone water-bowl. Coco looked at me pleadingly. My stomach twisted, as if I was seeing the prep-school dormitory where I would leave my first-born for the first time. I told Mrs D that I would ring in a fortnight and drove off.

October

'How's Coco?' I asked over the telephone, when I called. 'Not too bad,' said Mrs D. 'A bit full of herself, isn't she? Thinks she's leader of the pack, doesn't she? I'll see what I can do.' I relayed her opinions to my husband, who gave a hollow laugh. 'I can't think who Coco learnt that from,' he remarked.

Then he reminded me of our first attempts to train Coco, when I had sought the services of a society dog-trainer. She was tough and gorgeous, with a spiky crew-cut, and she wore leather trousers, with jangling chains hanging off them, and a denim jacket. She would come to the house. We worked on the basic commands – come, sit, stay and so on – and we would practise lead-walking in the challenging environs of the Portobello Market.

When it became clear that Coco would jump through any hoops for her expensive trainer, but utterly ignored her owners, we tried a special collar that sprayed Coco with limonella if she was disobedient.

My husband kept a lordly distance for the first few sessions. But then the trainer brought along her assistant. She was a Pre-Raphaelite slip of a thing, with the shy look of a wounded fawn. She wore long, bias-cut skirts, and clinging tops.

My husband was enchanted. He started being keenly involved in Coco's schedule and would begin to call me on my mobile to ask not where I was, for a change, but when we might expect the next home visit from the girls whom he had taken to calling, with a leer, 'Butch' and 'Femme'.

'Don't be irritating,' I would snap. 'They are canine professionals, not some lesbian music-hall double-act, and they are not called Butch and Femme. They are called Colette and Charlotte.' But it was too late.

When I was out, the dog-trainer rang and my husband couldn't contain himself any longer. He asked the trainer whether she and her assistant, who, he implied, were clearly sisters of Sappho and so forth, 'trained wives as well as puppies'. There was a pause. 'Yes I do,' replied the trainer to *le tout* Notting Hill, with a husky giggle. 'But you couldn't afford me.'

PS Go, Mrs D! When I went to get the new, improved Coco last Saturday, she was so sweet and obedient that I was really quite tempted to pick up the dog and check in the children instead.

November

November

What a red-letter day, eh! I came home to a card on our doormat, hand-popped through my letterbox.

'We are looking for a family kitchen to shoot a commercial for a well-known brand of cereal bar,' it read, and then asked me to call a number immediately.

I literally started gibbering as I thought of all the lovely money I'd pocket for the day's shoot – which could pay for Christmas presents – not to mention the lifetime's supply of free breakfast and brunch bars I'd get, in a medley of flavours and textures.

Though I rang and rang, the man from Frusli never returned my calls.

It's their loss, I told myself, as I do in these frequent moments of disappointment.

But then, funnily enough, I just received an email from an agent friend, also perfectly calculated to send the same frisson of naked, greedy ambition down my spine.

'Walt Disney Corp. is looking for a child to play the Youngest Heffalump in an animated series based on the Winnie-the-Pooh stories,' the agent alerted me. 'Upper age limit is eight. Oliver is the one, but the trouble is he can't read very well. Could you urge him to read more fluently out loud?'

Then she gave me the details. There was to be an open casting day, but if I thought Oliver had a particularly distinctive voice – 'a necessity, and they do love a lisp' – then she could arrange a 'phone casting' at home before the *Stage* advertised the role to London's pushy regiment of stage mothers.

Well, I have to confess I thought Oliver was right in there. He doesn't have a lisp, but he does have a husky, throaty voice that we find very winning. Anyway, I debated for about ten seconds whether to bribe him with his very own GameBoy if he could learn to read properly in the next forty-eight hours.

Then I did bribe him with his very own GameBoy if he could learn to read in the next forty-eight hours.

'A silver one?' he demanded. 'Yes,' I agreed. 'And the new Harry Potter game?' 'Yes, yes,' I cried. I mean, who cares when megabucks from Disney are dangling in front of one's eyes? The phone casting – I was beginning to pepper all my conversations with this phrase, along with the words, 'Oliver's agent' – was scheduled for 5 p.m. on Friday. Not a great time in our house, and frankly not enough time for Oliver to have learnt to read fluently, but needs must. So on Friday, at the appointed hour, I herded the boys into the playroom and the telephone rang. I was so nervous, I screamed. Then I came clean.

'Mike,' I confessed straight up (Mike was a nice bloke from the casting agency). 'Oliver, the seven-year-old with the husky voice? Well, he still can't really read, from a script.' Mike was great. Mike said that he would read some lines down the telephone and simply get the boys to repeat them back.

I leant against the door (so the dog and daughter didn't bust in) and we had Take One. My older son was supposed to be showing Oliver what to do. So he would listen intently to Mike on the telephone, then bellow out 'Don't come near me, you horrible monster' in a peculiar, stagey voice. He sounded like a Dalek. Oliver merely looked confused.

He carried on bellowing as I backseat-directed and said things like 'Expression, darling' and 'Your voice should go up at the end' and he glared at me.

Then he passed the phone to Oliver. 'Go on, darling, repeat what Mike is saying, just like Ludo was,' I instructed brightly. So Oliver whispered a few words inaudibly into the receiver. I grabbed the phone.

'Great, thanks, bye,' Mike said.

It was clearly a wrap.

'Not to worry,' said the agent who had first got my stage-mother juices flowing, as the weeks passed by without exciting news of a major offer from Walt Disney Corp. for Oliver's voice talents as the Youngest Heffalump.

'These phone castings are tricky. I usually get them to sing a nursery rhyme like "Ten Green Bottles" or "Polly Put the Kettle On". The last open casting with parents and children was for the lead puppy in *102 Dalmatians*, and, oh boy!' she sighed. 'The kids take it in their stride, but the parents! They can't help seeing the dollar signs flashing, can they, the poor things.'

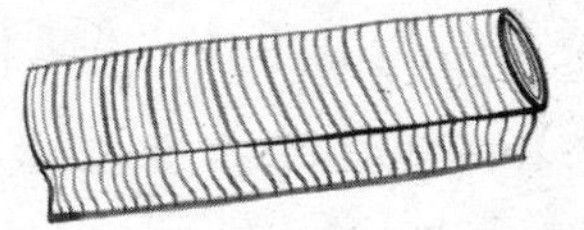

After we've done the morning drive-past, tipping children out of cars somewhere near their schools in busy streets, we Notting Hill mummies, I notice, are free to get on with the important business of the day.

Yoga.

At 9.30 a.m., you can barely spot a woman in these parts who is not purposefully making her way to some studio to tune her 'instrument' (it's what you call your body in Ashtanga class, darling), rolled-up yoga mat from Gucci under one supple arm.

About a hundred years ago, when I worked in an office (and the way I went on, you'd think I was running Estée Lauder single-handed), yoga was only practised by the sort of women who would knit their own children's bonnets out of lentils, and the pregnant.

Oh yes. I had my entitlement to 'antenatal care' and boy, did I make the most of it. On yoga days, I would sigh audibly and start tidying my desk. Wearing the faraway expression of the woman-with-child, I would leave early (this was in addition to all the time I took off for tests and scans, of course) to cross town to attend my 'yoga-for-pregnancy' class. The other girls in the class all had honey-blonde streaky hair and wore bootleg leggings and crop-tops, and were considerably younger than me. To whit, one of them was – permission to name-drop? – Jemima Khan.

I would roll up, sweating from the Central Line, and plonk myself as far away from her as possible, on the reasonable grounds that a seven-months-pregnant working mother of two who has put in eight hours at the BBC does not, actually, want to do the downward dog next to a *Tatler* babe weighing less than one of her big toes, even if Mrs Khan had had a particularly gruelling day sketching shalwar kameez.

'Anyway,' I would grumble to myself as I watched her tiny brown ankles emerge from her bootleg stretch-pants as she arranged her limbs in the lotus position, 'she's not pregnant. She's in the wrong class.' But week after week Jemima was still there, growing ever more lithe, glowing and vital. She looked as if she had, perhaps, swallowed a small plum.

One consolation of being in the group was that occasionally the instructor would call on *moi*, a childbirth veteran, to address the group, giving me a heaven-sent opportunity to reveal one of the unutterable truths about labour. (A bit tricky, actually: yoga dogma insists that giving birth is shelling peas, only easier, so long as you get the 'visualization' right. How I relished telling one of my gory birth stories to my captive audience of girlie *primagravidae*, as the teacher would try to cut me off in mid-flow!) Another consolation was my seniority. I would tell myself that if I was Mistress Frumpy it was because I was clearly so very much more pregnant than most of the others, and that I – unlike them, mere childbirth apprentices – had done this twice before.

Anyway, at the end of the two-hour session, the teacher would announce who in the group had given birth, where, how long it took, the baby's sex, and so on. And, as I said, Jemima was clearly Not Having A Baby. I had decided, in fact, that she must merely be keen on Liz, the teacher, who was rather marvellous in a bossy way. This particular class, I convinced myself, must be the only one to fit in with her hectic *Tatler*-shoot-and-shalwar-kameez schedule. But I still thought it was pretty selfish of her, frankly, as – I repeat – she wasn't pregnant, to take up a place in this particularly sought-after class.

November

As I heaved myself into the Life Centre one week, all of eight months gone, I gazed around the group and said brightly to Liz, 'Looks like I'll be next, eh?' Liz didn't respond – she seemed preoccupied by something – and Jemima wasn't there, but I presumed she was too busy being UNICEF ambassador to fit in yoga that week. Anyway, after the two hours, two long hours of meditation, omming, puffing with soft lips, exhaling through our vaginas, and so on, everyone was getting up to leave, flicking their hair and zipping up boots. Liz cleared her throat to make an announcement.

'Ladies!' she called out, flushing at the sheer wonder of her Good News. 'Just to say that Jemima had a little boy last night. Eight and a half pounds, no pain relief, just getting the breathing right [meaningful look around the group] and so a completely natural birth!'

Look, I know no one ever promised us a rose garden, but I found myself feeling more thoughtful than usual as I made my way home.

PS Other mummies: if Jemima's in your yoga

class, switch. She has babies without apparently going near the neighbourhood of pregnancy at all – perhaps she 'visualizes' them.

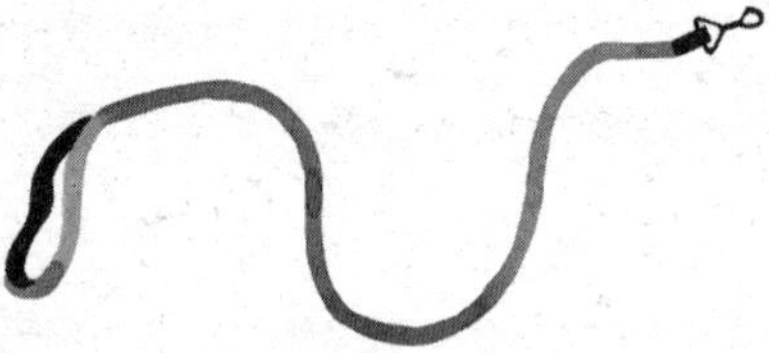

Where we live in Notting Hill, I am reminded this morning on my dog-walk (cheaper and a whole lot less competitive than yoga, frankly), my neighbours never appear to do anything they can pay good money to someone else to do for them.

I know that helping with their homework or preparing children for exams, for example, is often outsourced to private tutors or 'homework nannies'. There is one fashionable tutor who charges an eye-watering £1,000 a week near Common Entrance, and new clients have to wait for his services even longer than they do for the new Baguette bag at Fendi. (That's for five three-hour lessons, in case you're thinking of adding your name to the list.)

Anyway, as it's miserable outside I've just made a check-list of all the very basic services, as an aide-memoire, that no Notting Hill corporate wife should be seen dead doing herself.

1) Childcare: nannies, babysitters, housekeepers are de rigueur, as are weekend nannies and ironing ladies.
2) Cleaning: it goes without saying, we are much too posh to wash.
3) Gardening: and that extends to lawn-mowing, window-box-planting, sprinkler-setting, and plant-watering.
4) Washing the car: we leave that to a crew called the Three Valeteers, who will relieve you of considerable sums roadside to leave your inside trim as new.
5) Pet grooming: a mobile van called Pets in the City does big box office in our street, pampering pooches and shampooing pussies.

But these are only the basics, mind. If you are doing up a house round here, you don't just get the builders in – you have to hire, very conspicuously, an architect, a landscape gardener, a lighting designer, a telephony consultant, a hi-fi specialist who will pipe music into your bathrooms, and an interior designer. All their vans have to line up in a liveried fleet outside your house. It has almost reached the point where the only things that most women do without paying a consultant are unmentionable.

Take shopping and eating. You might think that these were two activities that even we Notting Hill mummies could perform without expert assistance, but you would be wrong.

Many women I know also have 'clothes consultants'. I should know: I've had one myself, I admit.

She came to my house, got me to undress and then model all the numerous fashion disasters (some still in their tissue-paper) that I had lurking in my wardrobe. She decided none of them were 'right for now' and bundled almost all my attire into three black sacks, loaded them into her car and dropped them off at Oxfam in Westbourne Grove, which is handily adjacent to Agnès B, in the expectation, presumably, that I would spend my children's inheritance there replacing all the clothes she had just junked.

But after spending money you don't have on tiny figure-hugging T-shirts and witty little suits, of course, you need frankly emergency assistance on the eating front, as all your new clothes from Agnès B are cut for teeny-tiny Frenchwomen, and will make you feel about as svelte as Anne Widdecombe.

Which means your next call will be to the Food Doctor, conveniently located on Holland Park Avenue. The Food Doctor is doing big business because thirty-something women like me just can't understand why our tummies jelly-roll over our waistbands.

Not wanting to accept that our condition is the very common one doctors must long to diagnose to their female patients as 'food retention', we trot along to the Food Doctor with our 'food diaries', in which we've meticulously inscribed all we've ingested for the past three days. And then the Food Doctor tells us not to eat – wait for this – 'anything white'. And for this vital service, he charges us a very reasonable £60.

'Muuum!' came the traditional howl from my daughter's bedroom early on Monday morning, as I was waiting to leave the house with her and Coco for the morning perambulation to her school in Notting Hill and the park.

'Where's my uniform?' 'In the usual place!' I screeched back, from the kitchen. 'No it's not!' 'Yes it is!' 'No it's not!' I like to keep things quiet and orderly on school-day mornings, don't you?

Then I had one of those wallet-patting, heart-lurching moments. On Friday night, I had stripped my daughter and bundled her entire uniform into the laundry basket. On Sunday night, I had been cramming yet more stuff in and glimpsed a warning flash of 'cherry' cardigan. So I had disinterred her uniform – gingham blouse, cherry cardigan, grey pinafore – and slung it into the machine, on quick wash. But then we had supper and started watching television, and so Milly's uniform was now a sodden, dark tangle in the drum of our washing machine, and Register was in fifteen minutes.

So why didn't I simply go to Milly's colour-coded closet and take out a fresh, ironed uniform for her? I hear Matron ask. Because she only has one of everything. And why does she only have one of everything? Because one blouse from Peter Jones costs £19.50. The pinafore costs £20. The hat, £8.50; the scarf, £12.50; and so on, till we get to the grey tweed double-breasted princess coat with velvet collar, a princessly £77!

It was awful, our uniform session in Peter Jones. I

can remember as a child the out-of-body excitement of going to Harrods, with my mother, to buy my first uniform for prep school, and thinking that my new electric-blue nylon rollneck, that clung alluringly to my puppyfat lumps and bumps, was possibly the most heavenly object in creation.

Milly's disappointment when I started sniping over the sheer cost of the winter uniform – I averted my gaze from the summer-uniform list, with regulation items such as 'straw boater with cherry ribbons' – was ghastly to behold. I was the Queen of Mean. I bought one of everything – and then only if it was compulsory. I refused to buy the hat, the scarf, the gym bag, the gloves. Though in the end I relented on several items, I don't mind telling you that I later rifled through the school's second-hand-uniform cupboard for the coat and accessories.

After this unsightly display of tightness in Schoolwear, I rang a friend, whose daughter had also just started at private school, for a moan. 'My boys have only ever had one of everything. It's all filthy by Wednesday, but that's too bad,' she agreed. 'When Flora started this term I got all her uniform from the second-hand cupboard except for the beret, which you have to get from Peter Jones for £15, and a pom-pom – another five quid – which you have to sew on yourself. Then another mother pointed out that actually even the second-hand stuff was jolly expensive so I took half of it back, so now she's only got one of everything like the boys.'

Luckily, man-made fibres dry jolly fast, so a damp and crumpled Milly and I were soon walking in a crocodile up to Notting Hill with all the parents and carers, to our various seminaries for young ladies and gentlemen of the parish. I invite you to picture the scene.

There were the boys, in their charcoal herringbone tailored overcoats, woolly Just William socks and caps and flannel shorts. And there were the girls, in princess coats, polished button shoes, pinafores and red pixie hats.

Then, of course, there were the mothers. For some reason, anyone escorting a child dressed like the Duke of Windsor or Princess Lilibet on their way to a state funeral can look instantly, through no fault of their own, quite frankly slobby. It's not helped, of course, by our early-day mummy uniform, which includes some of the most unflattering items ever to adorn the female form: trackpants, leggings, hoodies, trainers, and – please, no! – hipster jeans with visible thongs.

'I simply don't understand it,' said my mother when we picked up Milly later. She was staring in slightly appalled fascination at the parade of leisurewear at the school gates – a casual, sporty look hotly favoured by her own daughter. 'What a blatant dichotomy,' she mused. 'All the children are still wearing exactly the same old-fashioned uniform I wore *à l'époque* at Francis Holland – and berets, only ours were brown and we called them cowpats.' She tactfully refrained from comment on the mothers' updated uniform, which was probably just as well.

November

Sometimes I offer up a silent vote of thanks that very few outsiders have ever seen the shocking sight that is our family at breakfast, a scene of such kitchen carnage that it takes Barbara up to an hour to mop up after us.

When I get down, I find that the two older children have helped themselves to cereal. This is evident from the quantity of Cheerios littering the kitchen table, and the fact that I crunch Cheerios to powder everywhere I step. For some reason, the children insist on taking the inner bags out of the boxes (I think it must be to facilitate distribution of cereal over all available surfaces) and also on leaving their half-finished bowls in unexpected locations, where I find them crusted over later in the afternoon.

'Switch off the TV,' I call out weedily, as I take in the damage. 'Come and finish your breakfast. Tidy up your homework. Pack up your bags. Put on your shoes. Get your lunchbox. Where's your cricket stuff?' 'All right, all right,' they snap, crossly, emerging from the playroom, without, of course, bringing their cups and bowls with them. Then they stand looking mournful as I put on the kettle and start making the batter for Oliver's pancakes – and cooking bacon. And, sometimes, his fried egg.

OK, then, brief pause while I try to explain why, on a weekday morning, when the children have precisely forty-five minutes between opening their eyes to greet another gladsome day and leaving the house with the seven things they need for school (including something to do with volcanoes for show-and-tell), I am making a cooked breakfast for my youngest son – the child my mother-in-law described to me as 'not exactly spoilt, darling, more like ruined' at the tender age of eighteen months.

Well, breakfast is the most important meal of the day, for starters, and as Oliver doesn't appear to eat at school at all, I feel I have to stuff him like a Strasbourg goose if the poor child is going to last the day. And it doesn't, as I tell my scornful friends defensively, take all that long to whip up some pancakes and shove a tray of bacon in the Aga. But it's got to the point where having every single member of the family following their own special dietetic requirements from the à la carte menu at breakfast-time is adding to the already high levels of stress and mess.

If you must know, my husband and I each have muesli with blueberries and banana, half a grapefruit, and two cups of Lapsang souchong tea. My daughter has cereal, followed by some pitta bread with peanut butter, and hot chocolate. My elder son has cereal, followed by some pitta bread with jam, half a grapefruit, and any cold sausages he can find in the fridge. And Oliver has his stack of pancakes with maple syrup, crispy bacon, and a cup of tea.

After we have all finished, I avert my eyes from the table and start flicking through the paper, still muttering, 'Have you all got your shoes on?' and

'Leaving in five minutes' and casting apologetic looks towards Barbara, who is starting to tackle the Augean mess we have left behind.

The whole thing is ghastly to behold – but my worry is that it's been going on for far too long to correct now. My sensible and efficient friend Fiona, one of the few to have witnessed my chaotic breakfast session in person, has explained to me that the secret is to allow the children one bowl of cereal, period, and to hover over them as they finish it, whisk it away before they can ask for more and quickly put the bowl and spoon in the dishwasher. There is no tea-and-coffee service. No cooked breakfast. And certainly no pancakes.

'And then you have the weekend to have those long, leisurely breakfasts, when you ask who wants a boiled egg and who wants scrambled and who wants fried and all that,' she concludes. 'But not on schooldays – it's one bowl of cereal, per child.'

I may give the tough new *menu fixe* plan a go next week. But I'm not sure I will be able to resist when my hungry, ruined Oliver asks me for more.

November

Last weekend I grandly promised to roll out (as ministers say) my friend Fiona's plan to restructure the breakfast-delivery service in my area.

I'm afraid I have had to delay my initial report on the exciting new 'one bowl of cereal per child' scheme pending an unforeseen development.

We were burgled.

My wallet, containing Barbara and the cleaner's weekly wages, my credit cards and my mobile telephone were all stolen from the house (I was out walking Coco and the thief sneaked in, breaking down the French doors to the kitchen, in the half-hour window between Barbara leaving the scene and me arriving back from the park).

I have to confess that a small part of me has started to enjoy the post-burglary environment now that the chilling shock of intrusion has worn off and I've said goodbye to the fingerprints lady from Notting Hill Police Station, two police officers, the credit-card cancellation team, the people from Orange, and John, the locksmith from the security company who came to look at our flimsy doors, shook his head and said, 'So how long's them been like that, then?'

I was so grateful, you see, that the burglars hadn't spotted my laptop that I can only regard last week's burglary – our second since March – as a sort of deliverance. Had they taken the laptop, as they did last time, I would have been truly stuffed, because the day we were burgled was the day a bike from a publisher was arriving to pick up a piece of work, and that piece of work was sitting on a floppy disc in the laptop's drive as the footpads prowled around, and only backed up on the hard drive of the same computer. So, had they filched the laptop too… Well. I'm not saying it would have been perhaps quite such a crippling loss to literature as when T. E. Lawrence left the only manuscript of

The Seven Pillars of Wisdom on a train at Reading station (he had to rewrite his masterpiece from memory), but it would have been of marginal inconvenience to me.

So I am determined to see the silver lining in this episode. Firstly, it is quite relaxing being without my mobile phone, because if you don't have one – funny, this – no one can call you on it to ask you where you are, and brief you about their plans. Also, you stop checking to see whether it's in your bag or if you've had any missed calls. And you can walk your dog without thinking, 'While I'm walking Coco I could call Geoff and see how he's getting on with that quote for the barn doors, or reschedule Oliver's physio appointment, or call Fiona and see what she's doing later.' You just go for a walk, like you used to, in the old-fashioned Fotherington-Thomas way, where you actually look at things and appreciate their green and bosky beauty, instead of blindly seeing past them while nattering into space.

And secondly, it is a mercy being without my wallet, I have to admit. I told Barbara and my cleaner that I couldn't pay them. I cancelled my lunch in a restaurant, where I was taking Fiona out to lunch for her birthday, because I had no credit cards. I have not made any crazy impulse buys of fluttery skirts in local clothes shops. Until my husband came home the day of the burglary, I had to raid Oliver's piggy bank to buy milk, and I am subsisting on a drip feed of cash from him until my new cards arrive.

There is something atavistically reassuring about this level of simplicity. I do not buy anything except groceries, and I can't make frivolous and time-wasting telephone calls.

'I think this new system of you having no money of your own is working really well,' said my husband as he handed me a £20 note for housekeeping and left for the office. 'When your replacement cards eventually arrive,' he continued pleasantly (the post hasn't come at all so far this week), 'I think I'm going to confiscate them.'

December

December

I always approach end-of-term parent-teacher meetings with some trepidation, but this week my guys' verbal report-cards were spot-on. Oliver is 'on track' and also 'responds well to praise', his teacher told me, as I glowed happily.

Plus my daughter is very enthusiastic, and does lovely pictures to illustrate her work. In fact, the teacher and I admired some of them together and I went home on my bike whistling and full of festive spirit.

I mentioned my children's academic achievements later that evening to three girlfriends. A big mistake, as it turned out.

Nicky immediately confessed she'd just been told at her parent-teacher meeting – also 'in lieu of end-of-term reports' – that her son Ed, six, could do long division and long multiplication in his head. And that he needed special, individual homework assignments because he wasn't being 'stretched enough'.

'When his teacher told me,' she confided, 'I blushed. I felt as though she had just given me this huge compliment, and I felt like asking, "In what way am I so very beautiful?" It was really odd,' she said, fluffing her hair, in a ready-for-my-close-up way. Then she turned to Clare. 'But that's happened with all your boys, hasn't it?' she said, inclusively.

Clare's turn to share. 'Yes,' she admitted. 'They were both so bored in class – maths especially – that they were moved up a couple of years.'

How could I have forgotten? Just as, when you're pregnant, all the women you meet have had one of only two types of birth experiences – the baby either popped out like a ping-pong ball or the poor woman had a thirty-six-hour life-or-death labour – so it is when you meet mothers of London children of primary-school age. Their offspring have either been diagnosed with some expensive-to-treat learning disorder (dyslexia, dyspraxia or a hot new syndrome called perceptual delay, that our mothers and grandmothers would have translated as 'He's a little slow, dear') or they are gifted.

The final girlfriend to speak, Cass, couldn't really contribute because her son is still in nursery. But, to prevent her feeling left out, I assured her that it was plain to see that her three-year-old was special, too.

'The way he plays with his collection of Fisher-Price chainsaws,' I observed, as the others nodded in agreement, 'is quite remarkable.'

'Gifted. Definitely gifted,' we all chorused as Cass's eyes glistened with excitement.

And then, inevitably, my friends began comparing their offsprings' 'ceiling scores' in their private IQ tests (£250 a pop). Then we discussed whether all their kids were gifted in a *Royal Tenenbaums* way (great genes, dysfunctional family), a *Shine* way (emotionally stunted musical genius) or a *Beautiful Mind* way (schizo maths wonk).

I love my girlfriends, and their children, and this is certainly not aimed at them. But I'm starting to find this a tiresome new form of social exclusion/attention-seeking. If they're not trekking across London to take their children to after-school dyslexia centres, mothers are taking courses in how to parent their infant prodigies.

Look, I can see how satisfying it must be to be able to say, in a worried voice: 'Of course, now we've been told he's gifted, we're thinking Westminster.' But it does strike me that in the super-competitive world of London parenting, more and more children are getting pinned with either of these two labels.

Still, I have to say I wondered. In a neutral spirit of dispassionate inquiry (i.e., quivering with curiosity) I clicked on to the website of the National Association for Gifted Children, and completed the Is My Child Gifted? multiple-choice questionnaire for my Ludo and Milly. I had to answer questions on their reading, curiosity, memory, numerical ability and so on.

Even after I gave them some serious grade inflation (I answered yes yes yes to all the questions that shrieked Two Brains, like, 'Do they need very little sleep?' and 'Can they translate Greek iambics into Latin pentameters?', 'Do they invent complicated counting games?' and so on), the results still suggested that my guys fell short of the gifted mark.

I give you my honest word – I heaved a sigh of relief. But I still wonder why some concerned London parent hasn't set up a new organization – the Association of Average Children, say – for this newest minority group of minors.

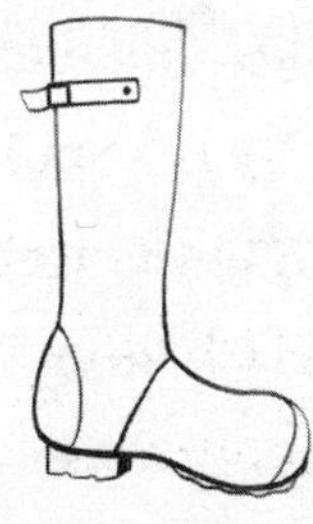

I was picking up my youngest son from school last week, when his new teacher, Miss Feldschreiber, spotted me and asked if I could wait behind for 'a quick word'. Now, I have been in the business too long to find this very alarming, even though I had just done three parent-teacher evenings on the trot, which I thought covered the waterfront. But still I scrolled through the options. Had he been kicking or – please, no – goosing the teachers? The school operates a system of debits and credits, but, as you might expect, I only get to hear about Oliver's 'credicks', not his 'debicks'.

'I think you should take Oliver to have his hearing tested,' Miss Feldschreiber said (and just try to imagine the porridge my son makes of that name). 'He's been awfully distracted! When we called him by name, he didn't even appear to notice us, did he?'

She appealed for confirmation to the teaching assistant, who verified that my son had been exhibiting signs of attention deficit.

I cannot pretend that this was good news. In my experience, schools are very quick to pick up on this stuff. Indeed, it was a Belgian Catholic state school, not us, that spotted Oliver's hypermetropia (meaning, he can't see very well).

December

He was peering at the blackboard, his teacher Mme Kremer told me one day, squinching her eyes like a sleepy hamster to illustrate her point. She went on, though, to announce that '*la service de sante scolaire*' was due to examine the children in *maternelle* the following week, and so, therefore, I should not 'derange myself'. I have Oliver's medical inspection, from a Dr Cochau, in front of me now, and it still reads like a vet's assessment of a prize heifer at a livestock auction.

They measured him (99cm) and weighed him (16kg). His spine showed '*bonne statique*' but they put two marks like this –)(– to indicate knock-knees.

His teeth were pronounced healthy, and the urine tests normal.

Then came the knockout punch. His vision at 5m was 'diminished'.

Now, thanks to the sharp eyes of Mme Kremer, he wears glasses, and his vision is getting better.

After Miss Feldschreiber's intervention, I whisked him to the doctor, a new young one.

She asked me whether he had been born at term,

and so on, and whether I had ever noticed him 'failing to respond'.

'But it's impossible to tell,' I explained, 'as a parent. You're always shouting, "Lunch!" or "Shoes on!" or "Time to go to school!" and they pretend they simply haven't heard.' I told the GP that no child of mine ever exactly 'responded', so it was difficult to establish whether this was profound deafness or deliberate cheek.

Then she looked into Oliver's eardrums, sighed, and said they were clean as a whistle. She said that, as the school had requested a check-up, she would refer us to an audiologist.

But I'm not sure we'll go. I have a sneaking suspicion that the problem could be mine.

A while ago, after a week of intensive swimming and sunbathing in Provence, I became completely deaf. I went to see my GP, who peered into my lugholes and said, with a slight shiver in her voice, that she could see 'waxy deposits'. Then she got a large metal syringe, which she filled with warm water. She handed me a kidney-shaped dish, and asked me very politely if I could hold it just beneath my ear.

She stood behind me and inserted the syringe into my ear. I had been tensed for agony but instead I felt a warm, flooding sensation. It was really rather pleasant. But then I felt a hand clutch at my shoulder, and heard a sharp intake of breath.

'What is it, Dr Bell?' I almost screamed (I couldn't see the contents of the kidney dish, obviously).

Dr Bell showed me.

While I was marvelling at the three perfect Maltesers I'd produced, she uttered an apology I will never forget. 'Sorry about that,' she said, gulping. 'But that was one of the most stomach-turning procedures I've performed in twenty-five years of general practice.'

Afterwards, I walked down Ladbroke Grove with my hands over my ears, because the loud report of my feet striking the pavements after this rather pleasant and effective 'procedure' was simply deafening.

With that in mind, I cannot help but pose the following deep, philosophical conundrum. When a child apparently fails to respond to a clear command, how can you tell whether it is because the child has not heard the question, or – in my case – the mother has not heard the answer?

I exercised the dog and children in Kensington Gardens last Sunday. I took them to see whatever it was – something Japanese and avant-garde – at the Serpentine Gallery, and then we watched the grown men playing with their remote-controlled toy sailboats on the Round Pond, which always cheers me up.

On the way back to the Princess Diana playground (near to which I had left the car), Oliver kicked Milly, who fell over. Milly kicked Oliver back. He fell over. Then Ludo kicked Milly, who cried because she hadn't kicked Ludo.

'Why did you kick her?' I shouted, as passing French families clad in matching Loden coats pursed their lips disapprovingly. 'Because she kicked Oliver,' he shouted back.

I ticked them all off and informed Ludo that we would not now be going, as planned, to the Rat and Parrot to watch Sky. I said we were going home and strode on, with them trailing in my wake.

But when we got to the Bayswater Road exit, Ludo had vanished. He had been sulkily loitering, but I thought he was following. He wasn't.

I got the rest into the car, and ran back. I toured the playground's perimeter, calling his name. I spent ten minutes searching. Then I realized what he'd done. He was walking towards Notting Hill Gate, to the pub with Sky Sports. On his own.

I ran back to the car and started cruising slowly towards the Rat and Parrot. A policeman and policewoman were passing. 'I've lost my son,' I explained.

As I said those four words, I could already hear the words 'To lose one child may be considered unfortunate; to lose two . . .' forming in my consciousness.

I was also reminded of Oliver's 'little walk' back in February, when he let himself out of our house, and half wondered whether the nice young police-couple had recognized me from last time. Still, I explained about the row, and the football, and the car, and Ludo vanishing. They took notes. They asked for a description. All the while, they were talking into their radios, passing on information. At one point, a police car drove past, and they directed it to the park.

'Just to brief you as to what's happening,' they said. 'We've got force from this borough and Westminster searching for him. We've got police combing the park. You're not to worry; there're hundreds of eyes searching for your son.' As soon as I heard those piteous words 'your son' I started crying. 'Mum's upset,' the policewoman radioed to the Met, and patted me.

Then, after what seemed like an age, her radio crackled. 'We may have located the missing person,' came the disembodied voice. 'We are stationary in a location by the Lady Di playground.' As I heard these words, I stopped whimpering. A helicopter thundered over our heads. Ludo had been gone half an hour.

We all jumped into my car, I did a U-turn, and headed back. A posse of panda cars nosed into the entrance ahead of us, and we ran towards the playground.

And there was Ludo, surrounded by five police cars parked at crazy angles and a large crowd of 'concerned' (i.e., gleefully rubber-necking) West London parents.

As I had occupied the resources of scores of police officers, five squad cars and a helicopter simply in order to find my son in exactly the place I'd left him, I started apologizing.

But my contrition was generously waved aside. 'We've all got kids,' the inspector said, as I tried to restrain myself from embracing him. Then he invited the children to ride back to 'the nick' in his car, and let them use the radio. When we got there, he insisted on taking all our mugshots 'for the noticeboard'. He gave Ludo a sign to hold under his chin with his name, date of birth, and the words 'High Risk Missing Person' on it, and gave me the Polaroid. 'What are you going to write on mine?' I tittered, when it was my turn.

'Well known to the police at Notting Hill,' he confirmed, and handed me a consoling cup of sweet Styrofoam tea.

One morning last week, I awoke to the sound of wailing and keening. I lay in bed, trying to work out why my youngest child should be making this piteous sound, and then I had what we home-working mummies now call 'a Cherie moment'.

My son's tooth had come out the night before. As I hurried him up to bed, I had told him how the tooth fairy would come and, in the morning, he would find some money under his pillow instead of his dear little yellowy-white fang.

'Waaaaaah! Waaaaaah!' he wailed, and I could hear the sound of his pillow and duvet being flumped around the bed. I lay there. I tried telling myself that the reality of my daily life was that, like Cherie, I was juggling a lot of balls in the air (don't you remember this little speech, delivered in front of cameras and with a moist eye, at the height of the flats-in-Bristol affair?). That sometimes the balls got dropped, especially at this time of year. That there just weren't enough hours in the day.

But I knew and Cherie knew that this was, frankly, a load of old balls. All I could hear was my son crying. The long and the short of it was that I had forgotten. I hadn't been wrapping presents and sending Christmas cards and basting the pudding with brandy; I had just gone to bed and forgotten. They should just line mothers like me against the wall and . . . help! Just as I was indulging in this orgy of self-recrimination, Oliver came snivelling to my bedside.

'Mummy, mummy,' he sobbed. 'The tooth fairy didn't come.'

'Yes she did, darling,' I said, with a bright, shining lie of a smile. 'She came and left you a pound but I was worried you might, um, you might not find it, so it's – ta-daaa! – on my dressing-table.'

The tooth fairy then waved her magic wand over my dressing-table and Oliver did find the coin I'd been pretty sure I'd seen there the night before. 'But why is my tooth still in the bed, then?' he asked. This was somewhat trickier to explain. But I thought it was worth the risk. 'The tooth fairy's got it, silly,' I said. Oliver went off grimly to check and, as I suspected, the tooth had vanished into the tangle of bedclothes.

I was in Starbucks the other day, and found an American writer friend looking particularly hollow-cheeked. 'Christmas, huh?' I commiserated. 'Mad, this time of year, isn't it? How we cram it all in,' and so on.

'You have no idea,' she groaned. Then she told me that she had flown in 'specially' that day from New

York, because it was her daughter's Christmas play at school.

She had taken the overnight flight in order to see her daughter perform. But, though she had written down the date of the show correctly, she had got the time wrong. She missed the final curtain by half an hour, she told me.

I tried to reassure her (she really did look racked with guilt) by telling her that I had missed prize-giving at my son's school by the same margin only last week. As I raced to the school gates, this flood of other parents was coming the other way, and several even stopped to congratulate me. Well, of course, my heart sank.

The one time I had failed to attend final assembly was the one time in his career that Ludo had actually won a prize ('most improved mathematician'), and I hadn't been there. And I hadn't been there not because I was juggling being a barrister and a consort and a charity worker and a mother of four, but because I had got the time wrong.

December

So, basically, I think that the whole juggling thing is a mother's Get Out of Jail Free card. Forgotten the school play? Left someone else's child on the kerb as you drive home with yours? Bought a flat in Bristol off a con-man? Didn't call your mother-in-law on her birthday? All you need to do is take out a small onion, hold it to your eye, gulp the words 'my son' and 'juggling' and all is forgiven.

Speaking of juggling and balls in the air, though, it has reached such a frenzy getting work out of the way, getting the presents to the godchildren, and doing my own Christmas shopping that I have begun to ring up all my relatives to request 'non-aggression pacts', whereby I promise not to produce any presents for them so long as they also, please, for Christ's sake, fail to produce them for us.

December

I was at the Sainsbury's checkout when my mobile went. I carried on unloading as I answered, scrunching my Nokia under my chin. He was somewhere in Scotland, shooting. 'I'm in Sainsbury's,' I answered, to the usual question.

'Look, sweetheart,' he said, in his most velvety tones.

'Yes?' I snapped. (Because I was in a supermarket on a two-trolley job the Friday before Christmas and my lifetime partner was engaged in field sports, I thought I could reasonably allow impatience to frost my usual warm spousal greeting-voice.)

'I'm in a taxi on my way to Glasgow airport,' he continued, 'and the thing is, the taxi-driver's got a PlayStation 2, still in the box, unused, and don't you think that will completely sort out the problem of what to give the children for Christmas? Only the thing is, if we want it, I've got to take this taxi immediately round to his house . . .' (Muffled exchange with Gorbals taxi-driver followed, of which I could only hear the words: 'Damn good bargain' and 'Yours for ninety quid'.) 'So whaddayou think? Quick. I need an answer, now.'

'Sweetheart,' I said, restrainedly, given a large and tutting queue was forming behind me, trolleys bulging with frozen turkeys, 'a PlayStation? I thought we were doing skates for all three and those walkie-talkies I've already got, from Argos, like I told you. What about our deal?' I hissed, as I tossed bags of clementines towards the checkout girl.

As I packed my shopping into 149 carrier bags, I felt a little bitter, for the truth is the mere suggestion my husband had just made had ruptured our enduring bargain, a compact that had lasted almost as long as our marriage, which was this: we would never buy the children a PlayStation or a PS2. Hell would have to freeze over first, etc. As we would both laughingly point out whenever birthdays and Christmases came round and the dreaded PS2 always headed our eldest son's list, not buying a PlayStation for our children was one of the very few things we have ever agreed on.

So, naturally, when my eldest son's birthday came round, as it did last week, I gave some extra thought to what to give him, especially since a PS2 was top of his birthday list as well as his Father Christmas list.

Obviously, I wanted to make sure that my husband was totally on side before we bought him his main present. Which I thought he was, until he headed off to the high street to buy the item we had settled on (a mobile crossed with a GameBoy called an N-Gage), while I did the school run from Hampstead to Notting Hill.

I was in the car with five children when my mobile, which I could not have on speakerphone for the obvious reason that the birthday boy was in the car, trilled. 'I'm in Dixons,' he announced, 'and they don't have it, so I'm going to the Link, where there's a sale on.' From the Link, I got a further call (he likes to keep me abreast of progress in real time if possible) to tell me that the N-Gage thingie was simply ridiculous, it cost £150, and that all games were extra. Then after what I thought was a lost connection, but turned out to be a pregnant pause, he revealed his fell intentions.

'I'm going to get him a PlayStation,' he said and rang off before I could issue my second veto in as many months.

And so he did. It was quite touching, I admit, to see my son open the present last Sunday on his birthday and watch him bury his face, pink with pleasure, into his hands with disbelief. Yes, I got a small kick out of that.

But nothing like the kick that my husband has been getting out of playing *The Getaway* (Platinum version) into the small hours, ensconced on the chocolate suede beanbag in the playroom, which makes me think there's something in this whole 'crossover' business after all. You know, the rash of things that adults and children can both enjoy, like reading Harry Potter or *The Curious Incident of the Dog in the Night-Time*, squabbling, or shopping at Gap together.

But when I came down late one night last week, having fallen asleep on the sofa, to find my husband carjacking the driver of a white van on Upper Thames Street, I did not comment that he had bought the

PlayStation as much for himself as for the children, because that would have been only stating the cruelly obvious.

As I now realize, he's been incredibly patient about waiting for his present for the past eleven years of our marriage. And as Father Christmas has so far brought me three healthy children and the dog of my dreams, I decided it would be unseasonally mean-spirited of me to spoil his fun.

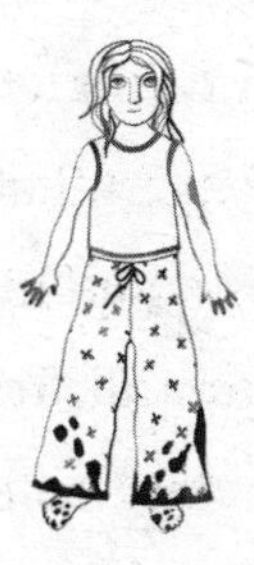

PS And on that note I feel I should explain why, so far, I haven't fully delivered on this book's subtitle. Eagle-eyed readers may have spotted that, over the year, I managed to lose my husband (to Africa), my eldest son (to the park, and he wasn't lost at all, but was merely waiting patiently for me to recover him)

and my youngest son (to the Portobello Road, when he wandered out of the house on Saturday and ended up in police custody). But I never lost Milly or Coco. Well done, everyone!

In mitigation, I am going to have to invoke poetic licence. The subtitle is a nod to the smash movie called *How to Lose a Guy in Ten Days* that you may or may not have seen (I haven't).

But there is perhaps a – deep breath – more serious point to be made, and just this once ('As it's Christmas,' as they say in Richard Curtis screenplays) I happen to feel like making it.

I am writing this postscript on my laptop at my beloved mother's bedside as she recovers from a rather gruelling hip operation.

As she always tells me, my boys will grow up and, in the vogueish phrase, 'move on' to find other mothers – sorry, I mean wives, of course!

And then a tear comes to our eyes, and we gaze at each other fondly. And we silently offer thanks for both our daughters, which for obvious reasons I find very moving and affecting.

December

When my mother sees my face, which is at this point contorted with profound emotion as I contemplate my astonishing good fortune in having such a wonderful daughter as Milly, she repeats her mantra.

'Boys leave, darling,' she says (and she should know – she's had three). 'But daughters don't.'

Which explains, I hope, why I and other mothers may, at times, struggle to keep tabs on our sons and our husbands. And also why I haven't been able to supply any amusing anecdotes whatsoever about losing my daughter and my dog (and Coco completed our family when Milly finally accepted that I could not provide her with an identical, twin, baby sister, so she's effectively a daughter too).

But I should add, as my mother does, this last thought (of truly world-beating originality, I know).

Whether they stay or whether they go, whether they are lost or they are found, you love them all the same.

Sniff!